A Swell Style of Murder

A Swell Style of Murder

by Rosemarie Santini

St. Martin's Press   New York

Design by Laura Hough

Library of Congress Cataloging in Publication Data

Santini, Rosemarie.
    A swell style of murder.

    I. Title.
PS3569.A546S9   1985   813'.54   85-10919
ISBN 0-312-78142-3

First Edition

10 9 8 7 6 5 4 3 2 1

A Swell Style of Murder

1

Rick Ramsey was jogging on West Broadway, the Fifth Avenue of SoHo, which gave a wide berth to tourists, taxis, and other appendages of success. But on this day there was not enough room for Rick, so he turned right on Prince Street and ran until he reached Mercer, a narrow back street fine to jog on. Hesitantly, he checked the pavement. Though the street offered more privacy, the pavement was a mess. For years, large trailer trucks had squeezed into the narrow space to deliver goods to the factories located there. Now the street was in the midst of a real-estate boom. Rick slowed down, cursing the pot holes and carefully sidestepping the bricks that had fallen from a co-op development, which covered practically the entire block. The sight of it made Rick sad. In 1964, when his family moved to SoHo, the hum of factory machines had driven them wild. They couldn't talk to one another until 4:30 P.M., when the factory day ended officially. Whenever he was in a nostalgic mood, those days seemed fun to Rick. But when someone else said, "Those were the days," Rick would shake his head and mutter, "Uh-uh, like it better now, no noise," just to be difficult. His wife, Rosie, said he liked being a minority of one.

Most artists hated SoHo as it was now and fought hard to

keep the past alive. They'd taken to the streets, painting angry signs on buildings like the Mercer Street Development, where thirty artists had been tossed out on the street to make room for a wealthy record producer. On one side of the building, Rick spotted a huge sign from that struggle. It was still visible, probably to remain so until the entire facade was sprayed. Nothing else could remove it, for rumor was that the sign was painted in blood. SOHO IS FOR ART AND NOT GREED, it read. It sounded to Rick like a late Sixties slogan, a period he had nicely avoided by playing football. Remembering the roar of his fans, Rick ran swiftly, like a deer, marking a pace not sensible for this SoHo street. He tripped and fell, face first, landing on the brick pavement, his nose wedged into a pile of bricks. When he opened his eyes, he thought he saw a hand. It was bloody and badly mangled. Rick let out a screech and shut his eyes. Then he opened his eyes and looked again. Yes, it was definitely a hand. A woman's hand. He knew that for sure because the long fingernails were manicured and painted blood red, matching the thick blood that was smeared from its mangled wrist. Four of the five fingers were covered with real jewels. Rick thought logically: This is not a robbery. Chilled, he realized that the hand must belong to someone who was dead. His body shuddered. He burst into a strange sweat. He'd bruised his lips on the bricks and a trickle of blood escaped from the cut, warming his chin. If I'm bleeding, then I'm alive, he thought, so he put his hands firmly on the concrete and pushed upwards. Miraculously, his body followed and he was able to rise to his knees. Unfortunately, he stole another look at the hand, causing his knees to buckle, leaving him flat on the concrete again. He tried to rise, but couldn't. Nothing was functioning. His well-trained body was failing him in a crisis. Rick couldn't understand that. He'd been trained since the age of ten to be a great athlete, which he was.

It was his father's idea. Major Ramsey had been a disciplined career soldier. When he'd retired from the U. S. Army, he became a sculptor, dragging Mrs. Ramsey from their immaculate house in Connecticut to a dirty industrial loft in SoHo to live illegally. The major grew a long beard and began sculpting larger-than-life statues out of old hardware. Because he believed in strong physiques, the major sent Rick to the Suki Hota Karate School. At age fifteen, Rick could lick any schoolboy. But Suki had also taught him Oriental philosophy. "It is the strength of the heart, not the muscles, that finally endures," he would often mutter while smoking an opium pipe. Rick took his master's word to heart and never fought with the Italian kids who called him Mophead because his hair was long. Instead, he ignored them, which made them furious. Often he'd arrive home with bruises and the major would go nuts. The beatings continued until he was sixteen, when he met fourteen-year-old Rosie Caesare. After that, the Italian boys were polite because Mario Caesare said they had to be. Rosie Caesare was now his wife.

Rick wished Mario was here on Mercer Street so he could tell Rick what to do. Rick felt sick. "No, I won't puke," he muttered. But he always felt queasy when watching a Steve McQueen film and now he was facing a dead hand. Suddenly, Rick screamed. Several passers-by looked his way and shrugged their shoulders, knowing that in SoHo, anything was possible. Few took the trouble to wonder why Rick was lying face down in the street, unable to move. As he lay there, he realized that the hand must have fallen from the roof. Maybe the body was still up there. Rick reached toward the hand and pushed it closer to him. It had been severed neatly. A professional job. Rick quickly pushed it back under the bricks, turned over, and vomited.

"You okay, fella?"

A trucker dressed in overalls was looking down at him. Rick did not want to attract too much attention at this moment.

"Too much jogging," he said, forcing a laugh.

"A way to go," the man said. He jogged on down the street and Rick realized he was not a trucker, but an artist in overalls. Maybe the hand belonged to an artist. Someone who wanted to make a point about art. Rick stole another look. The blood had clotted. No, this was not a fake dead hand. It was real. What should he do? He knew what Rosie would say. "Get the hell out of there fast!" So he did.

He jogged past the Alright Gallery, where minimalist art was making its last stand. Then he turned at the Fortunato Antique House, which was reintroducing the Marie Antoinette look, and ran quickly past the Sin Club, a new discotheque. Though it was early afternoon, strange types were already congregating on the long lifeline the Sin Club seemed to attract. He turned south, then stopped, slightly confused. A crowd of tourists was headed his way with a leader holding a bull horn. Rick resumed in a northern direction, heading for Houston and Broadway, where home was. He jogged slowly. Should he? Shouldn't he? Should he tell the police? Should he run right into the station in his jogging suit and say, "Look, well, I found a dead hand?" Or should he return and check the hand again? Was it really there? Why had he left the hand there anyhow? Shouldn't he have done something? He wasn't a guilty type. His police record was clean except for the two traffic accidents he'd had after his parents were killed in that plane crash. But he'd been in shock that day.

No, he'd done nothing. Rosie was probably right about him. His trust fund had ruined him. He lived in a strange world of his own making. Jogging to the health club every day. Loving his wife. That was his own sweet world. What did he have to do with a dead hand? No, he'd push it right out of his mind.

When he reached the pink building he called home, Rick sighed. Inside, the elevator car was waiting. He stepped into the car, put his key into the lock, and pressed the button. It was the kind of elevator where a finger had to be kept on the button to direct the car. But Rick's hands kept slipping off from too much sweat, and the car stopped and started abruptly several times. Finally, it reached the third floor and he quickly unlocked the loft door, which swung open right into the center of the loft. Rosie was standing there, dressed in a conservative skirt and blouse outfit. It was black, which meant they had company and it was family.

"Mom's here," Rosie said, quickly touching her security symbol, a red necklace that she'd spun about her neck several times. "And Aunt Irene's here, too."

Irene Caesare Campton, Rosie's aunt, was their landlady. She was a formidable woman. While Celia, Rosie's mother, was petite, Irene was chubby. Irene believed that the larger a woman's fortune was, the larger she should be. Irene was rich. She'd invested her late husband's profits from a small candy store into SoHo real estate. Now she was bleeding the artistic community and they hated her for it. Aunt Irene simply had no heart, claiming that living in Southampton had changed her perspective on life. Probably retired admiral Charlie Campton, her new husband, who had agreed to marry Irene and let her support him in her best manner, had something to do with her greed.

"Ricky, baby, how are you?"

Aunt Irene turned a fat cheek to Rick and he dutifully kissed her, retching from the taste of her thick rouge. Then he politely turned to his mother-in-law and bent to kiss her. "Hi, Mom," he said. Celia watched nervously as Rick jogged down to the kitchen area. The loft was large and open, and Celia could see all his moves from where she was sitting.

To the right of the elevator was a greenhouse where Rosie had planted strange herbs and plants, giving the loft a beautiful countrified air. In front of the elevator was a large space for sitting and talking. Rosie had placed three Victorian couches there, all velvet, because they reminded her of Bloomsbury. She'd mixed her favorite literary era, Bloomsbury, with her favorite film, *Casablanca*, by mixing the couches with cane-backed chairs. In the center of the potpourri was a round oak table cut from a large tree on the Ramsey property in Maine. On it were stacks of art books and parlor games. Off to the side was a large white grand piano the dealer had sworn once belonged to Lorenz Hart, Rosie's favorite lyricist. "A pure poet," she rhapsodized whenever she played his records. Rosie played the piano, but only when she was very happy. She'd taken lessons weekly because Mario had insisted on it, and had learned to love both Verdi and Lorenz Hart. On a wall next to the piano was a large poster of the jacket of Rosie's last book, *Sweet Dreamdust*.

Past the center space was a large kitchen area where an art deco half-moon counter with nine bar stools dominated, Rosie's idea of intimacy. To the rear was a large area with a dining table, which seated a dozen people. Rosie's family dined there whenever they came over, but the space wasn't adequate. There were always more Caesares than any seating plan could handle. They just kept arriving.

The dining area was very Italian. Reproductions of the Sistine Chapel were the wall motif. On the ceiling was a huge chandelier reputed to be from the Vatican itself. Rick knew the dealer had lied because he discovered a Chinese symbol on its inside. But he never told Rosie. Bordering the dining area were wide glass closets, specially built to display the various china sets that had been their wedding gifts. Though the Caesares had barely forgiven Rick for having married Sharon Neiman first, they could ignore that marriage because it hadn't been Catholic. When Rosie and Rick were dutifully married by Father Castora, crates of china and glassware arrived in their SoHo loft from the nine sisters and brothers who were the Caesare mainstream, and the various cousins, in-laws, nieces, and nephews who were secondary family. When it was all over, Rosie and Rick found they owned dinner service for one hundred people. Not knowing what to do with it, they'd hired a glass sculptor to design wall-to-wall cabinets to display china and glassware in a museum-like setting across one long wall.

At the other end of the loft was their bedroom. The door was shut tightly to deter any visitors.

Rick returned from the kitchen area, carrying a Coke for Rosie. He gave it to her and she smiled gratefully.

"What's the matter?" his mother-in-law said. She had small, intense, birdlike eyes which saw everything. Rick felt as if he were always being examined under a microscope when Celia was looking at him. He tried to be casual.

"Nothing, Mom."

"Ricky, I know you since you were young." She sat erect, pointing her finger at him. "Something's wrong. What's my daughter done to you now?"

Rosie shot her mother a fierce, angry look. These two did not get along.

"Nope, nothing." Rick hoped to avoid a family fight. He wouldn't be able to handle it, not today.

"You happy?" Aunt Irene chimed in. The women gave each other private signals. Like harpies, they began to encroach on Rick's private life.

"I'm happy. I love Rosie. Everything is fine." He tried to cover all bases, knowing Italians.

"So, why don't you have a baby?" Aunt Irene asked.

Rosie began playing with her thick red necklace and drinking Coke simultaneously. Rick knew he'd better put an end to this conversation fast or trouble was ahead.

"Uh . . ." he began.

"Mind your own business," Rosie declared contemptuously. She'd established her avant-garde identity years ago when she'd left her family home to live in sin with Rick and when she'd begun publishing novels with lots of four-letter words. But now that she was properly married, the women in her family constantly forgot that she was an independent woman. Instead, marriage had made her, again, an Italian-American daughter who could be questioned at whim. But Rosie kept fighting them.

Rick left the women and went back into the kitchen area, where he took a jam glass and poured straight vodka into it.

"Rick? What are you doing?"

His attentive mother-in-law jumped up, ran to one of the glass cabinets, took out a crystal stemware glass, and poured the vodka into it.

"Here," she said, "use this."

"My hands are sweaty. I might drop it."

"No, you won't," she smiled, commanding him.

Trembling badly, Rick gulped the vodka down. He'd begun thinking about the hand again and the vodka might help. Celia eyed him suspiciously, then shrugged her shoulders and went back to the other women. Rosie wore a stubborn look on her face, so Celia began on Irene.

"They did a good job," she said proudly, gesturing around the loft. Though they'd been here many times before, each time Irene and Celia would mention every new thing that the happy couple had added to the menagerie.

"I could have gotten two hundred thou for this," Aunt Irene exclaimed, her chubby fingers nuzzling the chocolate-covered cherries she'd brought. Irene had finished most of the box, her appetizer before a late lunch. "But your daughter was always my favorite niece," she continued.

Rosie tightened her hold on the red beads, so Rick sat next to her and took her hand. They'd heard this story many times. Aunt Irene had sold the loft to them for fifty thousand dollars, to be paid off in ten years with no interest attached to the deal. It had been generous and she never let them forget it. Rick squeezed Rosie's hand.

"I'm waiting though," Aunt Irene continued. She finished the last of the chocolates, threw the box aside, reached into her genuine lizard bag, and brought forth a linen handkerchief, wiping all remnants of chocolate from her chubby fingers. Then she delicately wiped the tips of her cherub lips. As she moved, her silk dress hiked up and her knees became visible, revealing dimples, which she patted with great pleasure.

"I'm waiting for that little baby girl who's going to be my godchild and carry my name," she announced, looking defiantly at Celia, knowing it was common custom to name the first daughter after grandmothers, not great-aunts.

Rosie made a strange noise and Celia, knowing her daughter well, decided to end the conversation with a truce.

"We'll see," Celia said to Irene. "But now, we've got to go."

Irene nodded. She picked up the lizard bag, which matched the tiny hat perched high upon her chubby head. Though it was early afternoon, Irene always dressed as if she were going to a cocktail party in 1946. Seemingly stuck in that era, she struggled up on her high platform heels, smoothed down her silk dress, and toddled toward the happy couple, looking as much like Joan Crawford as she could.

Rick and Rosie immediately rose to attention.

"Ricky," Irene said benignly. "Pull yourself together."

She kissed him quickly. When she turned to Rosie, her niece stared, challenging, but that did not deter Irene.

"Rosie, get pregnant quick!"

Rosie pulled away from Irene's moist kisses, but her aunt pretended not to notice. Her edicts uttered, she rang the elevator bell. Behind her, Celia gestured to the couple not to mind Aunt Irene and blew them a kiss. As she stood alongside the plumper Irene, Celia looked très chic, being appropriately thin, and dressed in soft gray Chanel-type suits with low Gucci pumps and bag, a contrast to Irene's glitter style.

When the elevator car arrived, it was operated by Max, the Abstract Expressionist painter who lived on the floor above. He hated Irene. When she stared at his unclean trousers, he smirked.

"Max? Are you going down?" Rick asked timidly, knowing that all the neighbors despised their landlady, Irene.

"Sure."

"Would you take along my guests?"

"Nope."

Celia smiled. "How are you, Max? How's your wife?" She gave him a maternal smile that would melt a rhinoceros. Max melted.

"Come on, then."

Irene waddled into the car with Celia following. After they disappeared, Rick locked the door with the double bolt. Then he slumped down on the couch and screamed.

"Jesus Christ!"

Rosie tore all her clothes off at once, standing finally in a hot-red bikini bra and matching panties. Rick eyed her.

"Baby, let's . . ." he muttered.

"Not now. I've got an appointment."

She raced over to the closet, opened the sliding doors, reached in, and began throwing clothes all over the place.

"Ugh," she said. "I've got to get some new duds."

"Baby . . ." he began again.

"I don't know why I do it. Those black clothes."

"You do it because she won't charge us interest if we keep her happy."

She nodded. "Good reason."

He grabbed her.

"Not now, Ricky."

"Rosie . . ."

"Hey, what's wrong? You're trembling." She stopped scampering about.

"I just saw . . ." He couldn't say it.

"Hmmmmm?" Her eyes looked confused.

"A hand. I found a dead hand."

"A dead hand?"

"Yes, a dead hand."

Puzzled, she felt his head quickly. Then she took his glass and smelled it.

"Rick? Have you been doing drugs again? I thought that was over when you left Sharon."

"On Mercer Street. It was a woman's hand. And it had lots of rings on it."

"You're not serious."

"Yes, I am. Do you think I'd make up something like this?"

She pursed her lips. "No."

"I don't know what to do."

"Don't do anything, for heaven's sake."

Rick looked at her. At this moment, he could happily strangle his beloved. Sometimes she took silly things very seriously. And sometimes, she took serious things too lightly.

Like now. She was trying to act macho, the way her father had taught her. Mario had informed Rick on the eve of his wedding to Rosie that he'd brought up his daughter to be courageous. "Like a man," he'd explained. "She's been taught to fend for herself." Rick had the feeling that Mario had decided to teach Rosie to act like a man after he'd realized that she was hopelessly in love with Rick. "It's not that you're not a nice kid, Ricky," his father-in-law often said, patting his stomach after a Sunday feast that included pasta, meat, mushrooms, brussel sprouts, salad, and lots of red wine. "It's simply that you weren't brought up to fight life. We Italians fight life from the day we are born. We know that life has to be defeated. That's why we are sexy and crazy." He paused a minute, his cheeks glowing. "We're really very simple." Then he pinched his wife and winked at her, making it obvious to all present that he found Celia sexual at all times. Rosie never had to wonder whether her parents were making it in the bedroom. They were. Rick thought that gave her an advantage over the rest of the world, all of whom, like himself, wondered how Mother received Father in bed. His father was military. Did he give commands? His mother never referred to sex and Rick wondered whether she knew about it. Often he thought about what his late parents would say about his decision to spend his life with an Italian-American Princess.

Rick jogged to the kitchen area, his running suit baggy from the pounds he'd lost. His Nikes squeaked on the polished floor as he stopped and searched the shelves for a nosh. Salted crackers? Did he want a heart attack? Health-store potato chips with no salt, flour, and no potatoes were his choice. He bit into one and coughed it up immediately. Health food tasted grim, but the chips were only ten calories each. Rick bit into another, opened the frig, poured apple juice into his mouth from the container's opening. Rosie wouldn't like that. She'd say it proved he was still living with his first wife.

Sometimes Rick would forget that he wasn't, but not when Rosie was in the room. Just the sight of Rosie in her orangy nightie turned him into a wild man. Under it, her nipples would shine through the silk. Her friendly, wide smile would reflect her dedicated camaraderie to the rest of the human race. Her green eyes would glow, especially in the dark when he pleased her in bed. At those times, she would forget about her firm decision that life must be endured with heroic stoicism. She believed that Freud was right when he wrote that life was all work and genital love. Rosie's own edict was that men and women were really brothers and sisters under the skin, not suited to mate, and that there was no point in expecting any kind of commitment from anyone. Whenever she sounded out her theories, Rick would feel a gnawing in his groin, an impossible desire filling his heart.

He would feel heartsick.

The problem was that Rosie wasn't heartsick. Tennessee Williams said it best in one of his plays: "You can't get heartsick, if you have no heart." Rosie claimed she'd lost hers in the eight years they'd been separated, while Rick was married to Sharon. Where a heart had firmly been lodged in her chest, somewhere between her magnificent Italian breasts, a replacement computer now existed. This computer balanced out what was good and what was bad, what was positive and what was not, how to deal with troubles, and most of all, how to be a success in this world of *new* women like Rosie, who somehow had forgotten all about romance and how to deal with *new* men like Rick, who were pushovers for it.

It was that kind of time. Everything had changed and there were no rules any longer. When Rick whispered to Rosie, "Let's make a baby," her gorgeous eyes would stare at him as she murmured, "Let's not." Part of Rick wanted to resist her charms, to hold out and state, "Stop taking that damn pill that makes most women crazy or I won't make love to you." But the other part, the bear that John Irving was always telling Rick about, took Rosie whenever and wherever he could. His wife was always ready. Every part of her would turn wet and soft. Her lips would part into a great sea of hunger. Then she'd part her legs with that same urgency, which made Rick immediately respond.

Rosie did not like foreplay. Whenever Rick tried to obey the latest women's sex manuals and make love to her slowly, she'd whisper, "No, too long. I want it right now. And fast, please." Rick forgot all the stuff about how to make love to the *new* woman and reverted back to Henry Miller, whispering "Do it!" as Rosie orgasmed loudly. Her favorite operas were by Verdi and, like this genius, Rosie did everything in great Italian chorus. Sometimes Rick did not appreciate this tendency, especially when lectured about the *new* marriage, the *new* couple, and the *new* woman. But in bed, her chorus fueled his fantasies. After making love to Rosie, Rick would sit patiently through one of her lectures, all of which he'd already memorized for his next life as a woman. And whenever he had too much, guilt kept him her prisoner.

He tried reality now.

"Rosie," he said, when he joined her on the couch, "you don't seem to understand. Down on Mercer Street, there is a woman's hand. A woman who used to be alive."

She jumped up from the couch and began pacing.

Exasperated, he got up from the couch and walked over to one of the china closets, opened the door, then fiddled under a gravy boat for his stash. The blue Gauloise container was slightly smashed, but Rick managed to retrieve one whole cigarette. He put it between his parched lips, went back into the kitchen, turned on the gas range, and bent his head, managing to singe his hair in the process. While patting the burnt hair, he quickly puffed on the cigarette, the smell of stale French tobacco filling the air. When he turned around, his wife was livid.

"Stop that," she commanded, hands on her lovely hips.

"It was a hand, Rosie. Try to get that word processor in your head to work. A real hand. You're for women's rights. How about women's hands?"

"Put that damn thing out." She stamped her adorable foot. But he puffed defiantly.

"We've got to go back there and get that hand," he said, narrowing his lips like Bogie. But he began coughing and the inside of his mouth felt like it had received several electric shocks by a KGB agent in a darkened cell. "No, no," he screamed. "I'll talk. You don't have to do that. I'm afraid of the dark. I'll tell you everything you want to know."

"You're really going nuts," Rosie commented.

Rick tried to answer, but his mouth refused to form words. He had a difficult time for a minute. She took advantage of his silence, pacing up and down in front of him, her arms crossed over her adorable bra. Whenever she swung about, Rick reacted to the lilting movement of her trim buttocks. What a bear he was. His erection grew. John Irving was right. Men are animals. Suddenly, he was struck with a sudden sharp pain and his vision shimmered with a variety of lightning bolts. Their intensity dazzled him and Rick knew he was hallucinating. He put the Gauloise out into a potted plant, one of Rosie's babies.

"Don't you dare, you ugly person. Take that thing and flush it down the toilet."

Rick couldn't move. Instead, he sat down on the sofa, feeling decadent and depressed. It was simply one of those days. He'd found a dead hand and he'd broken his two-year fast on smoking. He'd kept the Galouise in the gravy boat for an emergency. He knew Rosie would think him a weakling for that. Rosie didn't understand weakness.

She sat next to him and put her arms around him.

"Honey, honey, honey," she murmured and Rick remembered when he used the same technique on Sharon. What was Rosie lying about, he wondered.

"Look, darling. This is New York City. Things like this happen all the time."

"You're taking this too calmly. Don't you understand the hand was dead?"

She gave him a Mona Lisa look.

"Dearest, darling, Ricky, that's why I love you. You're a softie. With all those strong muscles, you collapse at the sight of a hand."

"You'd collapse too, if you saw it. It was all bloody

and . . ." Suddenly, the vision of the hand became real again. "Rosie, get a . . ." He tried to quell the upchuck that kept insisting it move from the pit of his stomach to his mouth. He didn't want to vomit on their new used Persian rug, but then he had no strength and his best intentions faded. Suddenly, breakfast was on the rug and he discovered that wheat germ did not mix well with Persian red.

"Oh, you poor baby," she said, kissing him.

Then she disappeared. Without her, he began shaking, but she came to his rescue, carrying a cold towel.

"Here, darling." She held it to his head.

He curled up, then put his head on her lap, where he felt safe. He never wanted to move from this place. He could feel the distant beat of her vagina, softly humming through her lovely panties. The feeling comforted him. Rosie tenderly soothed his forehead, cleaning his face with the towel. He was ready to die now. He was happy.

"We've got to go back and look for it." He remembered his duty too soon.

"No, we don't," she said.

"Rosie. Poor hand. What did it do to be cut off?"

"Rick. You don't want to get mixed up with this."

"With what?"

"With *those* kind of people."

"With what kind?"

Slowly, she reached for the *New York Post*, which Aunt Irene had left next to the empty box of chocolates.

"We were talking about it when you walked in."

"About what?"

"Read the headlines."

He picked up the paper and saw that, as usual, the *Post* had bold-type headlines announcing something sensational. He read: TWO BODIES FOUND ON SOHO ROOFTOP. The smaller type told him that the poor victims, a man and a woman, were found dead, minus their right hands. Rick put the paper down and looked at Rosie.

"So," she said grimly, "you've found one of the hands. I wonder," she added guilelessly, "where the other one is."

2

A slim woman waited in the doorway of a restaurant opposite the pink building. She had followed the jogger as he hurriedly ran home after he'd discovered the hidden treasure buried in the rubble on Mercer Street. It was exactly how she'd planned it. Now her lover would respect the person behind this mysterious act. Of course, he would never discover who it was, for she'd planned everything too well, down to each detail. Like him, she was a perfectionist.

The thick black sunglasses hid the woman's eyes as she thought about her lover. Her life was not unique. Like most women, she wanted love. And she had found a rare love. A passion. From the beginning, she had vowed to devote her life to her beloved. He enchanted her in every way. He was a man who knew how to make a woman happy. Many men had no idea about women, especially smart women like herself. She'd been impatient with all of them, but when she met him, she'd met her match.

She devoted her existence to him. Many women did not know how to love. They did not know that a passionate man could be enough.

But a woman must be strong to succeed. Her body was

slim due to diet and exercise. And she loved inventing sensuous games to keep him happy in bed.

Yes, the exquisite torture of passion was exhilarating to her. Everything became meaningless when he took her into his arms. She could not lose him, nor did she want to share him.

But he was a man. Men were romantic creatures, given to flights of fancy.

Not like women.

She was his goddess now and would do anything to remain so. Anything.

3

"Should we call the police?" Rick asked Rosie.

"Nonfiction really sells."

Rosie pursed her lips as Rick checked the phone book.

"I wonder which police station handles Mercer Street?"

"Miles said that nonfiction gets on *The New York Times* best-seller list faster than fiction does."

Miles Hamilton was Rosie's agent. Actually, he was *their* agent. Even though Rick had only one and a half stories written, Miles said Rick was a genius.

"For Christ's sake, I'm going to be thirty-four next April and I still haven't made *The New York Times* best-seller list. Erica Jong made it on her first book before she was thirty-three. Rona Jaffe was in her twenties. I've written three books and no soap."

Rosie was sipping a cup of ginseng tea, alternating it with Coca Cola. Even with Rosie's vitamin stress pills, her Life Extension tablets and health food, she still had one vice: Coke. She drank it all day long and sometimes all night. Often Rick fell asleep with fizz in his ear. Whenever he mentioned the noise, she would laugh and say, "Those bubbles keep me alive." Then she would grimace. "Coca Cola is making billions on poor idiots who gross out on the shit." Unfortunately, Rosie was one of them.

"Why don't we forget all about fame and go live in the country," Rick suggested. "You could raise vegetables."

"Ricky. How can you say that?" Her cheeks heightened with blushing indignation. Rosie looked like silk and Rick loved to touch her cheeks. His fingertips traced her lush lashes, following the shape of her oval eyes, but she grew troubled under his touch.

"How can you say that?" she repeated. "Don't you remember all the times I dragged you down to Canal Street so we could go to the Chinese movie theaters and make up words for the actors? Remember all the TV movies we watched without sound? I was always in training to become a writer. I've been in training since I was three, when Dad told me his stories. I didn't quite understand all of them, but I knew they were great. Growing up, I asked him to repeat them, but Dad kept changing the endings. Each time he did, it became more difficult to remember the first version. Now he says he did it on purpose. He was afraid the nuns were teaching me about heaven and hell, and he wanted me to know something about life. Besides, when he changed all those endings, he taught me a great lesson."

"What?" Rick asked.

"That life is unpredictable." She glared. "And that it can change at any time."

Mario Caesare had told his daughter stories about The Big Three: birth, sex, and death. He claimed that this is what life was and the rest of it—money, war, love, and so on—were all simply camouflage.

"Give it up. Maybe we could be happy," Rick persisted.

"That's the trouble with you. That money your father left has ruined you. It's not enough to change your life. It certainly isn't enough to destroy you. But it's enough to keep you lazy. You haven't done anything for months except sit on your sweet ass."

"I go to the health club every day."

Her look was completely hostile. "So what else do you do with your life?"

My God, Rick thought, she sounds like Gertrude Stein. Thank goodness she doesn't look like her. While Gertrude looked like a face on a cigar wrapper, Rosie looked like a Renoir. He leaned over and kissed her.

"Stop it! Why is it whenever I get serious, you get sexy?"

"Mario says sex is one of The Big Three."

"You leave my father out of this argument."

"Are we having an argument?"

"I'm trying to, but you can avoid fighting better than anyone else I've ever met."

His Rosie. How she wanted fame and fortune.

"Fame didn't make Sharon happy."

"Nothing could make your first wife happy." Rosie sipped the Chinese tea and grimaced again. "I've got to get to work."

"Take the day off."

"You're awful."

"Please. We could jog in the park. Just the two of us. Like a normal couple."

"Did Dostoyevski take the day off?"

"He drank and gambled. He must have gone out sometime."

"Did Hemingway?"

"He always knocked off for sex and swimming."

"Did Tolstoy, for Christ's sake? How about Colette? Did Virginia Woolf have lunch? And what about Carson Mc-Cullers?"

"She drank bourbon all day long."

"And Tennessee? Did he ever take a day off?"

"Losers. All losers."

"In life. But they were great writers." She said this with a ring of pride. Nothing meant anything much to her except writers and writing. That was first place. Second place was her

Italian family. Rick thought their marriage ran a poor third tied with her revenge about Sharon. Not like Mario's Big Three, but as heady.

"There are other things in life," he protested.

"What? For instance?"

"Kids."

"We'll adopt war orphans as soon as I have a best-seller."

"I want my own."

"Then have them."

"But . . ."

Her eyes filled with tears suddenly. "Can't you stop this?" she pleaded softly. Her head bent low and her hands trembled. "Why can't you stop this? You're supposed to be on my side. All you want to do is to turn me into a—a— woman."

"Baby, you are a woman."

"No. I'm not. Why can't you understand that?"

"You look like a woman."

"You men are all the same. You fall in love with us because we're different, and then you want us to roll right back into the baking pan and come out women. Well, we're not going to do that anymore."

"Who's we? I thought we were talking about you."

"We is women. We're not fools any longer."

"You're not happy either."

"How many people do you know who are happy?"

"I'm happy."

She snickered. "Ah-ha. That's the funniest thing I've ever heard. You're miserable. You sit around all day, knowing you should be doing something else, and then you go to the health club, where you rip *The New York Times Book Review* apart. You and those other losers who steam themselves all day long."

Then, suddenly, "Oh, I'm sorry. I didn't mean that."

"You meant it."

"I wish you didn't have the money. Then you'd have to

work for a living. That's the real difference between us. I have to work."

"You're compulsive. We could live on my money in the country."

"Damn it," she swore. "I want to make *The New York Times* best-seller list. Is that bad? How about a reprint sale of one million dollars? And foreign sales? The movie rights could go for . . . oh shit, why do you always make me feel guilty?"

"Rosie."

But once she got on a roll, nothing could stop her. "Then we could live in Europe. Maybe in France. Or Italy." Her eyes grew wide. "We could buy a Mercedes Benz. Green for me. Gray for you. And we could dump this dump."

"This is not a dump."

"And then . . ." Her expression changed. "Oh, what am I doing? Why am I talking to you? I should be at the typewriter."

"Stay a while."

"No."

"How's the new book going?"

"You know how it's going. It's going badly. Why do you ask me such nutty questions? Are you a masochist? Are you trying to turn me into one?"

Suddenly, she looked strange. He knew she'd thought of something.

"Since you discovered the hand, we could probably sell the rights to the story easily."

"Rosie, dearest." Rick was trying to remain sane. "The hand used to be attached to a woman. A woman who used to be alive. It's not just a hand, dear."

She soothed his brow. His beautiful Florence Nightingale showered tenderness upon him. With such warmth and love, what more could he want?

"Clean yourself up, dearest, and we'll go down there."

"What for?"

"We've got to get to that woman's hand before the cops find it."

"I don't want to do that."

"Ricky, we have to."

"Why?"

"We're in this together. Like Hart and Hart."

"A *Thin Man* rip-off."

She shrugged. "You're naive," she said.

"Idealistic."

"Naive," she countered.

"Look, we have to call the police. It's our civic duty."

Rosie stopped tendering Rick and put her hands in her lap. In this pose she reminded him of his grandmother, who would sit at her fireplace quilting. Grandmother Ramsey was a typical Connecticut grandmother, always filled with good things to do and say. She gave Rick most of the rules his life was based on. Fair play. Belief in the goodness and rightness of man. The fairness of the American system. Libertarianism. Equality.

Rosie had heard of none of these.

"Look, there's only one thing the Mafia kills a woman for."

"What?"

"Infidelity," she announced.

"But the *Post* said the man found with her was her husband?"

"What has that got to do with it?"

"You lost me, baby."

Rosie sighed patiently.

"She was probably getting it on with some Mafia goon and she was unfaithful to him with her husband," she said with a perfectly serious expression.

Rick sat up. Then he realized it was a mistake to sit vertically. From that position, he could see the mess on the new used Persian rug. He lay down again, crawling into Rosie's warm lap, where life was crazy.

She continued. "He probably wanted her to be faithful to him—all those Mafia types do—and when he probably caught her in bed with her husband, he probably got mad as hell."

"Lots of probablys. It doesn't make sense."

"Ricky, these people have their own sense. They have their own rules and regulations. Now, let's get back to us. We have to call Miles. We could get a book contract based on your discovery of the hand. I know it. Mafia sells books."

She babbled on happily. "We could do it together. Wouldn't it be great." She shook her legs joyously and Rick's head began rolling. "We'll do all the investigative work together. You've always wanted togetherness, now you'll have it." She gulped her words quickly. "And we'll challenge the police."

"Why are we challenging the police?"

"Silly. That'll make good copy."

"But it's not good ethics."

His pragmatic wife looked annoyed as Rick resisted her. This was a strange creature whom he loved with such abandon. Mario had created her with his truths, his stories, his examples of heroism, his indulgent love, and the end result was a courageous, manlike, very feminine, very sexual woman who fascinated Rick.

4

When Rosie and Rick decided to reside in SoHo after their marriage, they made a conscious effort to remain separate from the Italian community there. Though SoHo was Rosie's birthplace and Rick's teenage home, Rosie felt that family ties should be distant. The Ramsey-Caesare identity was that they were artists and that was where their loyalty should lie. Because of this, Rick wondered what the artists' community would feel about the dead hand he'd found. Was it a symbol of society's decadence? A threat to SoHo's peace of mind?

He wondered, too, what the hand meant to the Italian society he loved. Intrigued, he reviewed quickly what he knew about SoHo Italians. Very early on, Rick realized he'd married an Italian-American Princess. The Caesares were considered to be royalty because they'd earned the community's respect. This respect was not the kind Rick knew from *The Godfather Part Two*, when Al Pacino had trouble getting his wife to like him. No. This respect was hard-earned and involved Machiavellian twists and turns on life. The Caesares had prospered. Mario had begun his career as an olive salesman. Recently he'd retired, holding a stock majority in the company. After years of long hours, Mario now lived the enviable life of a European gentleman. He breakfasted at 8 A.M.

Chores and various business phone calls kept him busy till noon. Then, dressed elegantly, he would leave the house to lunch at an intimate restaurant. Afterwards, he would stroll around to Houston Street, down to Canal, up on Broadway, then across Eighth Street and down Sixth Avenue. He avoided with diligence Washington Square Park, though it held sentimental memories for him. It was where he'd courted Celia in the serene twilight. It was where he'd strolled with his daughter, Rosa, whose name was changed after she discovered she lived in America. Mario's park had been destroyed. It was now the center of vice and drugs. He'd predicted this terrible turn of events when New York University had decided to locate there. All Italians hated this campus because they did not like strangers. This distaste for the unknown was consistent throughout the Italian community, which was why everyone thought it quite odd when Mario had taken an instant liking to the then-sixteen-year-old Rick Ramsey. They'd whispered that it was because he had no son. Years later, after Rick had sinned with Sharon, Mario had forgiven him and allowed him to marry his precious Rosie, and even attended the wedding.

After they were married, the Ramsey-Caesare couple lived separate lives from the Caesare extended family. Rick and Rosie saw them only when assorted Caesares visited unannounced or at formal dinner parties. The remainder of the time, the couple acted as if they lived on the West Coast. At first, the Italian community was troubled by this, but later accepted it, because Rosie was a published writer and Rick had been a college football hero. They weren't sure what Rick did these days, but observed him daily as he ran to the health club. They'd nod to each other in a way that showed they thought he was a nice chap. He was now thirty-five. They'd known him since he was sixteen. After almost twenty years of observation, they were still making up their minds. But they were very nice to him.

Though Rick had this token acceptance, he never was privy to their confidence. He noticed that whenever he joined a group of Italians, their whispered conversations stopped cold. They'd always smile cheerfully and discontinue speaking. Were they talking about gangsters? The Mafia, perhaps? Rick didn't know. Whenever Mario talked about the Mafia, he said they were cruel beasts. Celia would plead, "Don't talk loud," even though they were generally at home.

It was clear to Rick that Rosie had been born into a hardworking, upright, moral, and very legal family, most of whom hated gangsterism as much as the late Robert Kennedy had. This is why Rick didn't really understand that the Mafia influenced every Italian-American in the SoHo community. And, more importantly, that the Mafia had a very direct influence on Rosie's character.

"Why do you need me?" Rick asked.

Rosie held his head in her warm hands.

"Darling, you must grow up. I love you the way you are, but if you don't grow up, I don't know what'll happen to us."

Instinctively, Rick knew that tears were not for now. Tears only worked when his wife was being unreasonable. When she was reasonable, she required action. He moved his hand toward her breasts, found a hot spot, and squeezed gently.

"Come on, Rick. Get ready. I'll call Miles."

The first person to learn about Rick's dead hand discovery was Miles Hamilton, the literary agent, who told Rosie not to call the police until he'd had a chance to call several book editors to see if there was any interest. He'd get right back to them. True to his word, Miles did get right back. Fifteen minutes later, his voice boomed over the phone. Rick was listening on the bathroom extension.

"Go for it," Miles announced. "I've got Melissa Adams at Bulloughs fascinated. I told her that this would be the great investigatory book on the Mafia. Rosie, you promise to reveal secrets, don't you, things that no one has ever told. Gosh, what a story. It'll sell to Spielberg or"—now, he whispered— "even to Coppola."

"Do you really think we should do this?" Rick asked Rosie after Miles firmed up the deal.

"Wear your blue turtleneck," she answered. Rosie had dressed in a gray suit, man-tailored and pin-striped. She wore flat pumps and carried a large safari bag that matched her wide-brimmed safari hat. She looked gorgeous. Rick kissed her.

"Hurry up, darling," she whispered, blowing hot air into his left ear, which caused him to slow down immediately.

"Let's . . ."

"Not now, sweetie," she said, licking his lips with her gentle tongue. "When we come back. Then we can celebrate."

Obediently, Rick turned to the closet. He was putty in Rosie's erotic hands.

Suddenly a thought shot through him. "Suppose it's not there."

"Huh?"

"Suppose someone else found it."

"Well, hurry up then."

"But . . ."

"Come on, Rick. You don't want me to go find the hand alone, do you?"

But he was bothered. He held out his hand with aplomb, gesturing for her to wait. Rosie paced as he picked up the *Post* and scanned the story again.

The bodies of Sally and Tony Salerno, residents of Thompson Street, were found on top of a SoHo roof this morning. Both bodies were fully clothed, but the right hands of both victims had been severed and were missing. A search is being conducted for the missing hands. The victims were strangled.

The bodies were fastened on a heavy clothesline by four steel clips, which the telephone company uses when repairing power lines. The building is an artists' cooperative, located on the corner of Houston and Lafayette Streets.

28

Lafayette Street? That was two long blocks from Mercer. How did the hand get to Mercer?

"Rosie?"

"I know. That's why the cops weren't around."

"The cops?"

"Yeah, the cops." She touched the brim of her hat nervously. "By now they've got the entire area roped off. Mafia is big news for the police. Are you ready, Ricky?" she asked impatiently.

Meekly Rick followed, sure that Rosie knew what she was doing. Naturally, the police would be at the scene of the crime. Rosie was smart. Adorable. Crazy. And his. He rang for the elevator car. When it arrived it shook strangely.

"Do you think it's safe?" she asked Rick.

"It's probably Arnoldo Agnew's electronic computer again."

Arnoldo was an expert in computer technology and often tested his genius on their loft building. They stepped into the car nervously. Rick held the button down. The car moved.

"Rosie, don't you think we should see your father and ask him about this first?"

She shot Rick an indignant look. "Why?"

"Because he knows about these things?"

"What things?"

He didn't want to say Mafia things. "About things to do in a crisis and things?"

"Rick, I can handle this. If you can't . . ."

"Who said I can't handle it? It's just that I've never had to deal with a dead hand before."

"Oh, dealing with a dead hand is like dealing with anything dead," Rosie said, very matter-of-factly. Rick watched her. In this crisis, she remained quite calm. Only the mention of his first wife could rile Rosie.

The elevator car landed with a thud.

"Damn Arnoldo," Rosie cursed, "someday he'll go too far."

But the elevator door wouldn't open. "More of Arnoldo's tricks," Rosie grumbled. Then she banged on the door. "Arnoldo, I'll get you for this," she shouted, knowing that his studio was on the top floor. Miraculously the door opened and there stood Arnoldo, holding a large grocery bag from Dean & DeLuca's gourmet store. Rosie picked up her safari bag and smashed it on the poor man's head. Arnoldo's groceries fell all over the lobby floor. Haagen-Dasz choco-chip mixed with Lum's black-bean sauce. Rosie quickly stepped over the mess. Rick hesitated. How could Arnoldo control the elevator while shopping at Dean & DeLuca's?

"How did you do it?"

"I left the computer on energy transport," he confessed. Arnoldo looked like Woody Allen, but could never capitalize on this resemblance because, unlike the film director, Arnoldo was six foot three inches and could never get anyone to feel sorry for him.

"Arnoldo, why don't you find a girl," Rick said, joining Rosie at the door.

"That was an awful, macho thing to say," Rosie accused Rick.

"Better than hitting him over the head."

"Was it, Ricky?" she challenged. "Sometimes action does more than silly macho insults."

He knew it was going to be one of those times. Only *mano a mano* would suit Rosie when she was excited. He'd seen her like this before. She was hot. It was the same excitement she'd felt about karate for women until her shoulders began swelling. Before she'd quit, he'd had to listen about karate endlessly, even though he was already a black belt.

"Come on then. Where exactly was it?"

"On Mercer."

"I hope the light holds," she said at the corner.

"What light?"

"To take shots. Miles said to take lots of photographs."

"Rosie, do you know what a mangled hand looks like?"

"I've seen this kind of thing before."

"What are you talking about?"

She sped up. Street hawkers were selling wallets, hats, gloves, shawls, and every kind of drug available to man.

"Look." She pointed. On the corner of Lafayette and Houston, the police had covered the area. Men in blue uniforms were running all over the place. There were several TV crews, an ambulance, and two priests. That meant the bodies were still around.

"Didn't they take them away?"

"Silly. First, they have to mark and measure everything, and look for fingerprints. Don't you know that?"

Sure, he knew it from films, but watching police on film and having it happen live was different for Rick. But not for Rosie.

Suddenly, he stopped.

"What's the matter?" she asked.

"I think we should take the police with us."

"Not until we wrap it up."

"Wrap it up. I'm not going to touch that hand."

"I mean take the photographs. Then we'll call the police."

"They might arrest us for interfering with police business."

"Ricky, show me where the hand is. Then you can go home."

"I'd never let you do this alone."

She blew him a kiss. "Sweet darling."

They raced down the street. When they came to the place where he'd found the hand, Rick lay down on the pavement.

"What on earth are you doing?"

"Reconstructing the scene."

"Oh, right."

He poked his nose about. No hand. Cautiously, he moved a brick. Then another. Had someone changed things? He moved another brick. No dice. Then he pointed his nose in a new direction. Still no hand.

"Someone might have found it."

"It's only been alone for an hour."

"There was a guy on the street. Maybe he came back."

"Keep looking."

He did. Then a brick toppled and a jewel shimmered underneath. It was the hand.

"Oh, oh," he moaned, feeling sick.

"Did you find it? Where is it?"

Nervously, he pointed. Rosie moved the brick with her foot.

"Oh, it's awful," she said. "Let me get the camera ready."

"Rosie, how can you?"

Camera ready, she pushed aside another brick. There was another ring—pearl, with ruby clusters.

"What awful taste," she said. He realized she was talking about the jewelry. She pushed another brick and there were suddenly five fingers visible. "Great," she said, and began taking shots. "Keep still," she said, hard at work.

Rick realized she was using the camera he'd given her on their honeymoon.

"What are we going to do after you're finished?"

"Wait a sec."

Click-click. The same camera they'd used during the idyllic time in Jamaica was now being used to take photos of a mangled hand. He couldn't hack it. Quickly, he struggled to his feet.

"Miles said we should call the police after we have all the shots because then the police will have to deal with us," she said proudly. "Since you found the hand, we'll have to be part of the investigation. That'll give us access that no other writers will have." Rosie hadn't flickered an eyelash while viewing poor Sally Salerno's bloody hand. Had he married a monster?

"Miles is smart. Ricky, we're going to make it to Hollywood this time." Satisfied, she stood there, hands on hips, proudly viewing the scene. "Let's see. Have we done everything," she asked as she put the camera back into her safari bag. Unsteadily, Rick leaned against her. "Ricky, don't faint," she said, absentmindedly, putting her arms around him.

"Honey, let's get the police."

"Okay." She looked at him. "Are you feeling okay?"

"Think so."

"Okay, then, let's get the cops."

But they didn't have to. They'd forgotten the first rule of detective work, to check out the location before doing their dirty work. When Rick turned around, he saw that a beefy policeman was glaring at them from a nearby doorway. He approached. A slender man in a tweed coat and hat, smoking a slim cigarillo, was with him.

"Uh-oh," Rosie whispered.

The slim man flashed a badge. "Hello, folks," he said calmly. "I'm detective Arthur Kushel. Now tell me. What were you two doing with that hand?"

5

Rick had never been inside a police station and had thought that "Hill Street Blues" exaggerated things. They hadn't. The East Sixth Street police station was gross. The station covered the east boundary of SoHo and part of the Lower East Side. In SoHo, with its *très chic* boutiques and classy restaurants, real-estate entrepreneurs indulged their greatest fantasies playing a sadistic Monopoly game with the Greatest City in the World, a fantasy that succeeded in changing each city block into gold bullion. But, as the neighborhood spread eastward toward Second Avenue, it became a junky haven. The Mott Street area had formerly been Italian, as SoHo had. While many SoHo Italians were forced out by greedy land merchants, Mott Street Italians had been pushed out by Spanish-speaking groups and drug dealers. Many people in the neighborhood worked hard, but unfortunately, many believed in the lifestyle of welfare-junk-jail, which is why the Sixth Street station was bedlam. At the entrance were several junkies, nodding out while waiting to be processed. When Rick and Rosie were led into the place, three gang members, wearing colors, were refusing to answer questions, quoting legal references far beyond their street comprehension. Two members of the Black Coats, one drug sect, were eyeballing two members of the Scorpions, another drug sect. Rick shivered, wondering how long this duel could last without an explosion.

Detective Kushel, Rosie, and Rick approached the desk.

"Yeah?" The old policeman who manned the front desk looked at the group.

"Questioning in connection with the rooftop murders," a beefy cop announced and burst into a smile. Suddenly there was instant attention from other policemen standing nearby. The Mafia was real police work. Members of the Mafia did not indulge in rhetoric, nor quote law books, nor have perennial body odor. The Mafia simply stared down the police, quietly waiting until expensive lawyers bailed them out. That's why an anticipation of pleasure could be seen on the faces of the law-abiding officers.

Rick looked around for Kushel, who had disappeared.

"Name?" the old policeman asked, holding a long form.

"Rick Ramsey."

"Profession?"

"Athlete."

"Writer," Rosie chimed in.

The old cop gave her one of those looks conveying that women should know their place. Rick knew this would cause discord.

"Writer," Rick agreed.

Several cops laughed.

"And yours?"

Rosie was brief and to the point. "R. Caesare."

"What?" Her inquisitor was puzzled.

"Mrs. Ramsey. She's my wife," Rick explained.

He stared at Rick.

"She uses her maiden name," Rick added.

"R. Caesare. How do you spell that?"

"C–A–E–S–A–R–E," Rick spelled.

"Ramsey. R–A–M–S–E–Y," Rosie spelled.

The beefy cop grunted and Rosie whispered to Rick, "Beefy." She motioned to the man.

"Kushel?" Beefy called.

"Here I am. We got a room. Come on then."

"What's the charge, Kushel?" the old cop asked.

"Suspicion of tampering with evidence," the detective answered. As he led them down a long hall to a small room, Rick protectively put his arm around Rosie.

"So . . ." Kushel began as soon as they were seated at a narrow table. The room was hot and stuffy, and it was painted a dull yellow. Someone had spilled purple paint in splotches on the wall, giving the place a look of grim discord.

"Could you open a window, please?" Rosie asked. "It's stifling."

"There isn't any window," Kushel explained.

"Could you turn up some lights?" she continued.

"We're having problems with our overhead lighting," he answered. "Besides, why do you want the lights on?"

Rick thought: probably because she wants to take photographs for the book. He glared at Rosie, but she ignored him. The room was in semi-darkness, a contrast to what Rick had been led to expect, having anticipated this scene from Hollywood's Forties' movies where cops questioned people with harsh lights until they sweated out the truth.

"Now, I ask again. What were you two doing with that hand?"

"I'd like to call someone," Rosie snapped.

"Afterwards."

"It's our legal right to call someone," she insisted.

"Not really," the detective countered.

"Look lady." Beefy was annoyed. "Pay attention."

"My name is Ms. Caesare. Caesar, with an 'e'," she retorted.

"Whom would you like to call?" Kushel asked pleasantly, signaling the cop to be quiet.

"My agent."

Silently Kushel pleaded with Rick, using his eyes to say, *Can't you control your wife?* "Afterwards." He repeated his edict.

"You haven't read us our rights either," she insisted.

"You're not under arrest," the detective answered.

"Yet," Beefy chorused.

Kushel shot him a testy look and Beefy fell quiet again. The door opened suddenly. A cop looked in, looked around, stared at Rosie, shrugged his shoulders, and left.

"What were you doing there?" Kushel asked again.

"I had discovered the hand and we went back to check to see if it was all right," Rick blurted. Rosie glared at him.

"Why didn't you call the police? We're interested in crime," Kushel said sarcastically.

"I didn't know it was a crime."

"You find a severed hand and you don't know it's a crime?"

"No."

"When did you learn it was a crime?"

"When I read the story in the *Post*."

"Why didn't you call the police then?"

"Because we're on assignment to write about this murder," Rosie announced. "Tell me. How did you know the hand was there?"

Beefy was about to say something nasty, but Kushel controlled the outburst by putting his fingers to his lips. Instead, Beefy stomped his feet. Kushel waited for quiet.

"Did you touch the evidence?" he finally asked Rosie.

"No," Rick said quickly. "I did."

"Don't you know that's a felony?"

"I'm sorry." Rick tried to look ashamed.

"Did you both touch the evidence?"

"No," Rick lied.

"She didn't?"

"She didn't have anything to do with it. She was with me." Rick smiled at his wife, who gave him the adoring look she reserved for whenever he did something wonderful.

"And what were you doing, Ms. Caesare?"

Rosie turned her full attention to the questioning detective. "It was obvious to me that the woman had terrible taste," she said. "Did you see those awful rings? Poor woman. Did she really die for love?"

"Mrs. Ramsey, please," Kushel protested, changing her

identity at whim. He turned to Beefy. "Can you get me a tuna sandwich and black coffee at the machine? I haven't had lunch yet."

"What a terrible way to eat. You should have something nutritious," Rosie began, but Kushel silenced her.

"Look, Mrs. Ramsey. I'm tired. I've been up all night."

"Were the bodies found last night? The *Post* didn't say," she pursued.

"Yes," he admitted wearily.

"Who found the bodies?"

"Ahh . . ." He stopped, suddenly aware of Rosie's tack. "Look, Ms. Caesare, did you know the Salernos?"

"No," she said. Rick nodded in agreement.

"Your maiden name is Italian. Where do you come from?"

"I was born in SoHo."

"Mr. and Mrs. Salerno lived on Thompson Street. You must have known them."

"No. I didn't."

"Ms. Caesare, I've worked this precinct for a long time. It's impossible if you were born in SoHo and are Italian, that you did not know the Salernos."

"Well, she didn't," Rick said, annoyed at Kushel.

Detective Kushel looked wiped out as Beefy returned with lunch. Beefy whispered something to Kushel and Rick heard the words "dago chippy" and prayed that Rosie had not. To his credit, Kushel waved Beefy away. Then, under Rosie's scrutiny, he ripped open the wrapping on his tuna fish sandwich. Rick checked the time. It was 4 P.M. Poor guy, Rick thought. How awful to wait for lunch. Everyone was silent as Kushel chomped on the sandwich, grimacing his distaste for it but forcing it down with gulps of black coffee. Rosie shook her head compassionately several times, but Rick was glad she did not lecture Kushel on the merits of good nutrition and the possibility of early death from tuna fish right at this sensitive moment. The tuna fish sandwich was half eaten when Rick heard a familiar sound outside the door. It was a thunderbolt. A great burst of deep shouts. Rosie looked up. They locked stares. Then she looked down, a dreaded look of anticipation on her face.

Suddenly, the door burst opened.

"This room is taken," Kushel said nonchalantly. When the man in the doorway did not go away, Kushel looked up at him.

Mario Caesare stood there, observing all like a ferocious tiger about to spring. He took in Beefy, who had begun walking toward him. He measured Detective Kushel's measurements. He looked at Rosie, checking to see if she was okay. Then he looked at Rick with an expression of pure rage.

"How dare you . . ." he began.

"I—" Rick started to answer, then realized Mario was talking to Kushel. Rick bit his lips nervously.

"How dare you bring my daughter into a shit place like this?"

Kushel was staring at Mario with disbelief. Behind Mario was a well-dressed man whom Rick had never seen before. Graying at the temples, his taut blue eyes stared arrogantly as he opened his Gucci attaché case to produce a sheaf of papers, which he gave to Kushel.

"I'm the attorney for Mr. and Mrs. Ramsey. Andrew Carnego. This is a writ of harassment signed by Judge Carlson."

Beefy swore under his breath and Mario shot him a *dread* look, one of Mario's specialties.

"Harassment?" Kushel was puzzled as he groped for an eyeglass case, which was sticking out of his left breast pocket.

"How dare you?" Mario said again, using his dread look now on Kushel.

"Mr. Caesare." Attorney Carnego tried to calm Mario.

"I'm not harassing anyone," Kushel said, relieved when he read the writ. "I'm simply asking questions. These two"— he pointed to Rick and Rosie with malice—"were found at the scene of evidence in a double-murder case." He paused for breath as Beefy cursed again. Rosie looked up at the cop, annoyed, but kept quiet. Rick took his cue from his wife and stayed mum.

"Harassment!!" Mario shouted. "My daughter will sue you!" He turned to Rosie. "Come, darling." He motioned to the door.

"Wait a minute," Kushel warned.

"Look." Mario looked at the slender detective with pity. Though he was not a large man, Mario gave that impression under duress. "Do you want trouble?"

"Mr. Caesare, your son-in-law touched the evidence."

"He didn't exactly," Rosie chirped in, but her father glared and she was struck dumb again.

"My daughter is not going to spend one more minute in this place. Do you understand me?"

Kushel didn't understand Mario, but trembled as he held his ground. "No."

Mario's body began to swell. Suddenly, the buttons on his well-tailored suit busted. The collar of his silk shirt from Florence tore as his neck muscles bulged into a mass of red flesh. The nostrils on his fine slim nose bellowed out, and a strange hissing sound began to erupt from them. His cupid lips, generally pleasantly posed, tightened and drew into a malicious knife-like line. His hands grew into bubblegum bursts of tendons and veins. When his Gucci belt buckle snapped off, he was almost ready. But, before he could act, another man appeared in the doorway. He was plump and sported a large mustache. He spotted Mario's readiness and smiled at him knowingly. Mario hesitated.

"Detective Kushel?" the newcomer asked.

"Yes, Captain."

"Do you have any hard evidence here?"

"Circumstantial, but enough to question, Captain."

"Then I suggest you question the Ramseys at home."

"At home?" Kushel's eyes popped. Beefy began stomping, but everyone stared at him so he stopped.

"Unless you have very hard evidence, Kushel, Mr. Caesare doesn't want his daughter to be in this station. I'm sure, as a father yourself, you can understand his strong feelings."

"Yes," Kushel muttered. Beefy's face deepened in color; it was now purple and about to explode.

"Now, I think we can safely let the Ramseys leave with Mr. Caesare," the captain continued.

"What—" Kushel started, but the captain's mustache began turning up at the ends and Kushel shut up quickly. "Mr. Ramsey, when will it be convenient for us to question you and your wife?" Kushel asked nicely, amazing Rick.

"Anytime," Rick said, trying to be equally polite.

"Call first," Mario announced, then snapped his fingers and everyone rose to attention. Mario's tan summer suit blended nicely with Rosie's pinstripes as he wound his arm protectively about her. "Come, darling," he said. To Rick, he added, "Hurry up." Rosie looked at Rick sadly, then was led from the room. Rick followed. He knew by the folds in Rosie's forehead that something was about to happen. Outside a long black car waited. Three minutes later, the car arrived at their loft. Silently, Mario got out of the car, escorted Rosie out, and Rick followed.

"Thank you, Andrew," Mario said to the lawyer.

"It was nothing" was his polite response.

They walked into the lobby and Rick was happy that none of their strange neighbors were around. Feeling lucky, Rick pressed the elevator button and the door opened immediately. As the car rose, Mario glared at Rick. It was going to be a bad time, Rick thought, as he held the button for their floor.

"Okay, let's all sit down calmly," Rick suggested when they arrived at the loft.

"Rick, I want to speak to Rosa alone."

Rick stared at the older man. He'd heard about Mario's famous temper, but he had never seen it in action, especially not directed at Rosie, whom Mario always handled like rare, exquisite lace.

"Rosa?" Rick mumbled.

"Can you leave us, please?" Mario said.

"Huh?" Rick stood there.

"Go out for cigarettes."

"I don't smoke."

"Then go out for a beer."

"Don't think I should."

"Let him stay, Dad," Rosie said.

"It's not possible."

"Let him," she insisted.

"No," Mario insisted.

"I'll stay," Rick insisted.

He went to a cupboard, took out several glasses, then went to the frig, where a bottle of Moët was chilling for a special occasion. Rick thought this might be the right moment. When he opened the bottle, the cork hit the ceiling loudly. Champagne soaring, Rick's spirits lifted too. He poured and served Mario, who waved the glass away. Rosie drank hers in one gulp, which was odd because she never consumed alcohol. Mario looked at Rick, then shrugged his shoulders hopelessly. Apparently he'd decided that Rick would not cause too much trouble after all. He turned to Rosie.

"So what about it?" he asked.

"Rick found the hand. My agent says we could sell it as a book."

"A book?"

"Poor hand," she said, wrinkling her forehead. She glanced at her father, smiling wanly, trying to melt down his fury. "It has no body, that poor hand. The poor woman. Some beast did this to her. I know it."

"It's not your business to know things like that."

"I know who did it," Rosie insisted.

"We both know who did it."

Rick sat down quickly, weak at the knees. Were they finally going to mention *them?*

"Look, Dad," Rosie began.

"Don't Dad me," Mario said. Then he paced the area, stomping on the Persian rug. "Where did you get this?"

"At Atwoods," Rick answered.

"Crap," Mario decided. "Why didn't you go to my friend's place. You could have gotten wall-to-wall."

"Dad."

"I'm not your dad, I'm your father."

"Father, please don't carry on like this."

"Rosie." He turned to her, his dark eyes opened wide, his cupid lips dripping with tenderness. "I'm a good father, aren't I?"

Quickly, she nodded. So did Rick. He was amazed that Mario had rescued them almost as soon as they'd entered the police station. How could that be possible? He'd heard of the Italian grapevine before, and now that he had seen it in action, he was dumbstruck. He coughed nervously when Mario glanced at him with contempt.

"I want you to listen to me," Mario continued. "Stay with those books about sex and modern women. The filthy books."

"Dad, they're not . . ."

He waved her comments aside. "Write about the West Coast. Write about Detroit. Write about Texas. Get a job on 'Dallas.'" "Dallas" was Mario's favorite television show. "But never write about New York. Got it?"

"I have to write about what I know. Miles says that's when I'll be a best-seller. It's a question of intimacy. That's my writing problem. I'm writing about things I know only from research. I want to write about something I know from life."

Suddenly, Mario's face turned calm as he sat down next to Rosie and took her hand in his, his love apparent in his tender looks.

"Sweetheart. There are things that are too sacred. Like your family. You can never write about your family. You know that, don't you?"

Rosie's beautiful eyes were filled with tears. Rick wanted to cuddle her as he watched her nod her head obediently.

"And SoHo. You can never write about SoHo. You know that, don't you?"

As she shook her head defiantly, her green eyes shone like emeralds in sunlight. Rick swore to himself. Rosie was beautiful when she was determined.

"But it's not about us," she answered stubbornly. "It's

not about real Italians. It's about those beasts. It's about time someone wrote about them the way they really are."

"Not you. Never you. I don't want to see my daughter's body on a slab."

"They don't kill writers these days."

"Who says?"

"They didn't kill Puzo."

"He was lucky."

"They like the attention. *The Godfather* made them glamourous. They love the media now."

Mario shook his head. Then he tried another tack.

"What about your respect for the Salerno family?"

"I—"

"You know they're in terrible grief. Do you know there is a child involved? A beautiful girl. Do you want to spread her sadness, this *infamita*, all over the papers—you, my own daughter?"

"It's going to be in the papers anyhow."

"Yes, but not written by an Italian."

"Lots of Italians are reporters, Dad."

He shook his head, disbeliving. "But not you. Not my Rosa. Never my Rosa."

She shook her head too. All her life, she'd been trying to carve her own identity. Hadn't he taught her to do that? Rosie turned to Rick. "Darling?"

Rick agreed with Mario, but for very different reasons, although they were equally cowardly. But he had to stick by his beloved or she'd never forgive him.

"Mario—" he began.

"Stay out of this, Ricky."

"Rosie's my wife, Mario."

The older man nodded, knowing that a husband and wife should never be interfered with and that he was breaking one of his very own rules.

"Rick?" Rosie's voice broke.

"Look, Mario. Rosie and I . . . we're writers. We have to tell the truth. But we'll be careful. I promise you."

Mario shot Rick the dread look. Then he began pacing

again, walking up and down in front of the velvet couch from his daughter's Bloomsbury fantasy. He smoothed his forehead with nervous fingers. "I want you to stay out of it. Everyone will know who you are. I don't want anyone to think that we could cause anyone else pain. Besides, the whole community is upset."

"It's upsetting—" Rick began, but Mario cut him off.

"You don't understand. You see, now that the woman's hand has been found, she will be buried in sacred ground. But her husband . . ." He smacked his forehead with his own hand. "Her husband can't be buried until his hand is found. So he's being kept on ice, which isn't nice."

"Why can't they bury him without his hand?" Rick asked.

"Because they can't," Mario answered. He put his hand in his pants pocket, took out his gold key chain, and twisted it about his fingers, the clashing keys causing a brassy sound. "Look, I said I want you both to drop this."

"We can't," Rosie said.

His eyes were misty as he turned to her.

"Look, Rosie, I won't be able to take care of you if you do this."

"Yes, you will, Dad. I know you."

He looked at her carefully, his gray-green eyes searching hers. She looked like a cheshire cat, a look she'd practiced before a large poster of the Mona Lisa which faced the loft's toilet facilities. It was there, while tending to bodily functions, that Rosie perfected the picture of mysterious passion that she sent her father now. He understood and nodded. Then he left without saying good-bye. They'd made some kind of settlement and though Rick had been privy to it all, he didn't know what on earth had happened.

6

The slim woman watched Mario leave his daughter's loft. This man might be a problem because he was from the old school. He knew the ins and outs of things. He would never have left the severed hand in the street like his son-in-law had. No, Mario would have immediately gotten rid of the hand, knowing that its discovery would lead to intense police harassment in SoHo.

Funny. No one would suspect why the hand was left in the rubble. The police were a joke. And the Council would not want to get involved. No one knew that her lover's favorite fantasy was World War II with bodies and limbs strewn all about the streets of Rome. He was a child then and he had never forgotten those times. Somehow, they were immersed in his passionate feelings.

She wondered when the other hand would be discovered. Well, it was still missing. She had hidden it well. She walked to her car. Her head was covered with a black hat; her face was unreadable under wide black sunglasses. She liked it that way. She wanted to be invisible. It was the best way to keep an eye on everything.

7

"Mom says that Sally Salerno wasn't always the way she is now," Rosie said as Rick nibbled at her ear.

"Of course not, silly. She's dead now."

She shot him an indignant look. "No, that's not what I mean."

"What do you mean, honey?"

He held her close as they spoke. They were in bed. The sun was shining brightly and the bedroom wore a cathedral air. The sleeping enclave was bare, with a long, wide mattress on the floor and, next to it, a statue of the goddess Ishtar, one of Rosie's favorite women in mythology. On the walls hung several large paintings by friends. They were mostly abstract nudes, Rick had been told. Several framed posters were scattered in odd wall spaces, mostly of the Impressionistic French period, Rosie's favorite era for fun art. Since Rick's taste in painting ran rather gothic and gaunt, he let her decorate their site of love.

Above the mattress, on the ceiling, was a large mirror. Rosie said it was nice to see reflections at all times. Rick stared at his body. He knew that people said he looked like Tom Selleck of "Magnum" television fame. He would agree, except that his eyes were clear blue and Tom's were . . . what were

Tom's? Rick hadn't checked that out, yet he knew their eyes were different. Rick kept his body in terrific shape. And his legs weren't bad. He lay there, admiring what he saw above.

"Stop looking at yourself," Rosie complained. "That mirror was put there to enrich our sensuality, not your vanity."

"I was looking at you."

"No, you weren't," she laughed. "You have a different expression when you look at me."

He changed his focus and concentrated on Rosie's body. God, she was pure and perfect. Her legs were long and slim, but curvy in the right places. Her hips were soft and round, yet slim. Her waist was tiny, but her breasts were very full. Her neck was like a swan's, long and graceful and curious. And her face. God, her face drove Rick wild. It was as if all the French Impressionistic and Italian Rennaisance portraits were smelted into one beautiful face: hers. Rick found it difficult to choose his favorite feature. Her eyes were large and oval, their color changing from jade to emerald. Her nose was slim and small, but fluffy, too, like a Spanish dancer's. Her cheeks were high, her mouth was pouty and always begging to be kissed. Rick turned and kissed her, losing himself in time.

"How do I look when I'm looking at you?" he asked later.

"Funny. Like a soft kitten. Your eyes grow larger and larger, and get drippy wet like a baby's."

"And . . ."

"When you look at yourself, your chest heaves, like you're proud of what you see. Funny, I can always tell. I wonder whether Sally could tell too."

"Tell what?"

"Tell what her beast was thinking."

"Obviously, she couldn't tell or she wouldn't be dead."

"Not necessarily." Rosie's eyes slanted.

"What do you mean?"

"Uhh." She shook her head, then went on. "Poor woman. Mom says that she was quite beautiful when she was younger. She ran away with a don's son in Sicily. Do you know what a don is, Rick?"

"A count?"

"Kind of. Well, it caused a scandal because she was only fifteen and he was engaged to marry a rich girl. His father cut him off without a dime and they came here. He became a gambler. Everyday he'd dress up in fancy clothes and go to the various clubs to gamble for their living. That's how he got to know those beasts."

"Was he one?"

"Nope. When their baby was born, he asked Sally what she wanted in return. She said she wanted him to get a job. So he went straight to the post office and became your average door-to-door mailman. That was his life. He went to work at five in the morning and got home at four in the afternoon. Sally waited at home. Everything was fine, until one day some beast spotted her. She was even more gorgeous after she became a mother."

"That can happen. Who was it?"

"This beast," she answered, avoiding all clarity, "sent his men to her. He offered her money, jewelry, anything. He'd fallen in love with Sally immediately. He was Sicilian and that's how they fall in love. Remember *The Godfather*, when Al falls in love with that village girl?" Rick nodded. "That's how Sicilians fall in love. Fierce." She shook her head nervously. "Well, she still refused and he kept bothering her. She went to Church and told Father Castora. Father sent word to the beast that Sally was a good woman and that he shouldn't bother her any longer. But the Church never registered much with Italians."

This had always fascinated Rick. "Why not?" he asked.

"Don't know. Dad says Italians only think of the Church three times in their lives. When they're born, when they get married, and when they die."

"Isn't that odd?"

"Not at all. Italians believe that everything should have

its proper place and the Church gets out of hand if you give it too much attention."

"I think it's because the Pope lives in Rome. My grandmother used to tell me that whenever she would talk about Catholics."

"Protestants never understand," Rosie said arrogantly, annoying Rick.

"Why don't you explain it to me then?"

"You take church too seriously." She waved away his heathen curiosity.

One of the reasons Rick liked being a free-lance writer was that he could research projects in the oddest places. Like now, they were researching their project in bed and the publisher would never know.

"What happened then?" he asked, knowing that Rosie had heard the whole story from Celia.

"Well, the beast wouldn't let up. He finally figured a way to get to Sally. He told her if she didn't agree to see him, he'd have her husband killed."

"Ugh."

"You're right. That did it. Poor Sally. Because she loved her husband and wanted her daughter to have a father, she agreed to meet the beast for cocktails. And then it happened."

"What?"

"She fell madly in love with the beast."

"How come?"

"It happens." She shrugged. "Who can tell why and how. I don't know why I fell in love with you, I remember when it happened."

"When?"

"It was when I was trying to learn the skateboard and fell flat on my nose. I was bleeding and you picked me up and wiped off all the blood. Then you carried me home. Before you rang my bell, though, you kissed me."

"Yeah, I remember."

"Remember what Dad did when he answered the door?

He hugged and kissed you for taking care of me. And he gave you lots of candy. Sour balls, wasn't it?"

Rick nodded his head, remembering.

"That's when I fell in love with you."

"I thought it was when I took you to the prom and brought you orchids. That's what you always told me before."

She laughed. "I lied."

"Why?"

"Because I wanted to save the true story for a moment like this." She turned toward Rick and kissed him. They caught fire. His hands snuggled under her armpits and he lifted her over him. Then he kissed her face. Her silken skin nourished Rick. He kissed her hair. He could feel his excitement grow as she stroked his body. Her hands felt like the softest wisps of the wind, tingling, touching, taunting.

"Rosie, I love you so."

"I love you, too."

Then her body opened up to him like a hot and humid jungle flower, and her arms held him as large petals would. He wound her body around his middle, exploring her orally, noting that her perspiration tasted like peppermint tea mixed with ginsing. He began hearing harsh beats on a drum, thudding louder and louder, and realized it was his own heartbeat. He listened, waiting for her signals. "Now," she moaned. He entered her, familiar with the way her body would move gracefully to accommodate him and then, how her body would thrust against his, causing exquisite torture. She sighed, then moaned, as he penetrated her, first slowly, then harder until they could not breathe evenly. Their lips touched, hot, parched, and a hissing sound came from hers. He opened his eyes, wet from love. Through the haze, he watched their two bodies in the mirror above them. They were closely entwined, like the statues of love surrounding Roman villas.

"Now," she pleaded. "Now. Now."

He shook, then lost himself inside of her, beating, pounding, heartbeats slamming with passion, harder, louder, until they shivered with love. Then moans became one moan, whispers one whisper.

"Oh, darling," she gasped.

"Baby. Baby. Baby. Oh, baby."

Finally, they rested.

"Promise you'll always help me to stay open and eager and wild and curious," she said.

"I promise."

He kissed her warmly.

"I want to be with you always."

He took her trembling hands in his and kissed the fingertips, one by one.

"Promise me that we'll grow old together and that we'll always be artists and always live in SoHo and always lead exciting lives," Rosie said.

"I promise." They kissed. "But what if you become a best-seller?"

"What do you mean, if?" She glared. "Besides, what about it?"

"Our lives might change," he said gently.

"Nope. Besides, we'll both be best-sellers. That'll even out things. The trouble with you and your first wife, whose name I shall not mention, is that she was the star and you were the escort." She paused, pondering her next move. "Besides, the real trouble was that Sharon was a pig."

"She wasn't."

"She was. Admit it. All that cocaine she took. Those pills to wake up. Those pills to write with. Those pills to get to the hairdresser. For God's sake, did Sharon take pills for sex? And what kind?"

"I don't want to talk about Sharon."

She curled up in a fetal position, then her toes were saying hello to his toes, cuddling them.

"Tell me about sex with her."

"What's to tell?"

"How did she like it? On top. On the bottom. On her side. Oral. Or anything else special?"

"She liked sodomy. That's what Sharon liked most of all."

Her eyes brightened as she urged him to continue.

"I don't know why, but she did. She said she'd learned to like it in Spain. It's a form of birth control there. And then, when she toured South America, she really got to like it. So that's what we did. I made love to the back of Sharon. I never saw her eyes."

"Grrrrr . . ." Rosie hissed. Then she looked at the mirror, speaking to Rick through his reflection. "Did you like it?"

"It was okay. I mean, anything's okay once in a while, but she was determined never to change position."

Rosie's eyes glittered in the mirror as she smirked.

"I wonder what she's doing now. No wonder she went with a German count. He probably taught her the fine points of sadomasochism. And her Spanish bullfighter. If he had all those kids, he couldn't like sodomy. I wonder what happened with him?"

Rick began getting angry. "Lay off. I don't want to hear any more about her."

"Why not? Ashamed?"

He turned to Rosie, grabbing her harshly. "I'm not ashamed of anything I did with Sharon. After all, we were married."

Her face contorted. "Yes, but you didn't really love her."

"No," he agreed. "I didn't. But I was fascinated by her. To men, that's the same thing. Once cocks get hot, that's what we go for. It's simple. We're ruled by our erections."

She cuddled him. "Not really. Men are ruled by their hearts like women are. They just don't know it yet."

"Are you going to teach them?"

"No," she laughed. "Only one. There's only one man I'm interested in."

She put her arms around Rick again and held him close, nuzzling at his neck. Rick warmed up, and kissed her.

"But . . ." she interrupted him. "Why did you finally leave her?"

"I don't want to talk about it."

"Come on. We've been together for a while now. We have a solid marriage, don't we? We're going to write a book together. We have equality. We have the loft. We're secure. We can talk about her." She spit it all out at once.

"You won't like to hear this."

"Let me be the judge of that."

Rick held his breath for a minute, then plunged in. "I left Sharon because she added a new wrinkle to our sex life."

Her eyes opened wide. "So . . ." She waited eagerly.

"She tried to get me to sodomize her with another fellow watching."

"What?" Rosie screeched, sitting upright. "Did you ever do it?"

"Not really."

"Did you?"

"Only once."

"What did it feel like?"

"It felt the same way as when I saw the dead hand."

8

Her head burrowed deep into the pillow's pure silk. As always, after he left her, his touch was deeply etched into her flesh. Now she hugged her body, a temple of his worship. The flush of love was upon her and she treasured it. Her love. Her darling love.

But she had to get dressed and could not linger in bed. She walked into her luxurious bathroom. Last night he had lit the scented candles and they'd made love in the perfumed bathwater. She had swept his body with reverent kisses. He, in turn, had explored every part of her body with parched lips of desire. Without him, she felt like a desert cactus; with his touch, she blossomed.

Carefully, she showered. His scent was still in the room. A black parrot sang a jungle song. He'd given her the parrot and placed it in a gold gilded cage next to the sunken tub. The bird trilled, blinking his eyes as he performed. She smiled as she worked on her body. She used a special cream for her skin. Last night, she had painted her face like a Berlin whore in the days before the Nazis. Now she spotted a shimmering rhinestone still pasted on one breast. Last night he'd been delighted with the rhinestones. Then he'd described his fantasies of the women who collaborated during the war. Afterwards, he told her, their heads were shaved. Good. Now she had something new to surprise him with.

Carefully, she shampooed her hair. Then she dried it. She loved her long locks. All throughout childhood she'd worn long braids. Now her hair fell to her waist, covering her breasts.

What would he do when she surprised him as a wild creature of the war? She trembled with anticipation.

Quickly, she prepared. First, the scissors. The long tresses fell to her feet, shimmering in the light. Then she picked up the razor, began working and chunks of hair fell to the floor. She soaped her scalp and shaved her head. Then she opened her robe and shaved carefully. Soon, all her vaginal hair was gone too.

She checked her reflection in the long mirror. Her body was soft and clean, like a baby's without any hair. She knew this would thrill him.

She smiled. How private their secrets were. The world never suspected. Her wardrobe contained perfect wigs, large hats, and exquisite turbans. Now she walked into the large dressing room and selected a gray silk summer dress with a matching turban. Then, before a meticulously neat dressing table, she perfected her makeup. Afterwards she slipped into the dress. Underneath she wore no underwear. She placed the turban on her shaven head. Then she slipped her feet into gray sandals. There. She looked elegant.

When she returned to the bedroom, she spotted a package on the chaise lounge. She loved to find his things. Curiously, she looked inside the bookstore bag. There was a book with a smashing pink cover. The title was *Sweet Dreamdust*. She leafed quickly through the book and noticed that it was terribly sexy. She laughed. So he liked reading about sex, too. She glanced at the photograph on the back cover and was startled to see a beautiful young woman: Rosie Caesare. The book had been written by that reporter, Mario's daughter.

Suddenly she remembered how eagerly he had awaited her arrival last night. He was sitting in his robe. As she entered the room, the robe fell aside and she saw that his penis was fully erect. At the time, she'd thought he'd been anticipating her arrival. But now, she remembered he'd put the book down when he looked at her and said, "Get naked."

She had. Then her lips had taken his passionate organ.

Now she examined the photograph of Rosie Caesare suspiciously. Had his passion been aroused by her or by this photograph? Angrily, she tore off her turban. With her right hand, she felt her scalp, her supreme sacrifice for his love.

But she would do anything for him and there was more to be done. She kicked the book to the floor, put the turban on again, picked up her bag, and left the house. Soon she was on the highway to the city.

The drive did not take long. When she arrived in SoHo, she parked opposite the pink building. In a phone booth she dialed Rosie's number. A man answered. The husband must be home. Quickly, the woman hung up.

9

Rick looked at the engraved invitation, which read: AN EVENT AT 5 P.M. AT THE ALRIGHT GALLERY.

"Get ready," Rosie called from the shower. But Rick had his daily pushups to do. He began working out as memories of that Prince Street space interfered with his concentration.

Tatania Sirlanki's Alright Gallery had formerly been an illegal Chinese fortune-cookie factory. As a teenager, Rick wondered whether the fortunes were put in before or after baking, but no one would tell him. The Chinese were secretive, like the Italians. On his way home from school, he'd often sneak into the factory to watch the Oriental women with their feet bound in heavy cotton to keep the floor clean. The Chinese were very clean. Even as they sweated, the women would hurriedly wipe their faces dry. They would sit in a row, mixing batter, forming cookies, putting them on a large sheet pan. At the rear were huge ovens where two women would stand, pushing the sheets in and out. Often, when the oven doors opened, the hot air would blow the women off their feet. Calmly, with wonderful stoicism, they would stand up and wrestle again with the heavy metal until it shut tightly.

The illegal factory was bought and became the Alright

Gallery, one of the first SoHo galleries. Whenever Rick went there, he saw the ghosts of those women, dutifully working, heads bent, putting fortunes in cookies for Americans. This memory haunted him even though Tatania Sirlanki had transformed the space into an elegant maze.

The floors and walls had been stripped and polished to a shiny gloss. In the center were several pure white silk couches and lots of pillows. Rows of spotlights hung from the ceiling, focusing on the walls. But the huge ovens were still there. Tatania had transformed them into objets d'art.

Tatania had been born in a small town in Hungary, where her family had owned the largest house and one male member had always been Mayor. When the Communist government confiscated her house and land, Tatania confiscated the family jewels and fled to Paris. There, she met painters, poets, and writers who later moved to SoHo because lofts were large and cheap. She went with them.

Immediately, everyone noticed her because Tatania was built like a wrestler. She had a ready smile and laughed all the time except when she drank vodka and sang melodic songs about love's slavery. Not knowing what to do with herself, Tatania decided to become an intellectual. She published three books about her life, but they did not sell. Undaunted, she cashed in her jewels, bought the fortune-cookie factory, and went into the art business. She created six "events" each year, all guaranteed to set the art world on fire. Whenever she drank vodka now, she did not sing melodic songs about love's slavery, but, instead, lamented that Hollywood had never filmed her life, though it was stranger than fiction.

Tatania was planning an "event" that she promised would be fabulous. She was introducing a painter from Puerto Rico. Carlos was short, and sensational in bed. Tatania wanted to give him something in return. Carlos wanted nothing. He lived in a hut at the beach and painted all day long, stopping only when too tired to go on. Then, he would drink wine, eat fruit, and have whatever woman was handy. He was happy, poor bastard, but Tatania would soon change all of that. She imported Carlos with his large canvases and announced an "event" that she hoped would begin a new era in art.

"Thirty-five. Thirty-six." Rick's pushups were getting to him.

"Rick? Are you ready?"

"Yup." He jumped up, his sweatsuit grimy. Rosie stood in a robe, looking at him.

"You're not ready," he noted.

"Are you wearing that?"

"Uh-huh."

"WASP!"

"Everybody dresses down for Tatania's so the uptown people can feel comfortable."

"What are you talking about?"

"The collectors. They've started coming to openings in sequined running suits."

"Rick. Are you really going to the event looking like a pig?"

"Okay. Okay." He conceded.

Actually, he wasn't a real slob, but in training to be one. But he would never make it; his Connecticut background haunted him whenever he tried to be slimy. He showered, then shuffled along to the closet with a towel wrapped around his waist. There, he chose a white linen suit, dark blue shirt, white tie, white straw hat, white shoes. dark blue socks, polka-dot shorts. Once dressed, he waited for Rosie.

"You look wonderful," his wife muttered as she made her grand entrance dressed in elegant black silk.

"You're not going like that!" Rick shouted.

"Why not?"

"Because, my love, I can see your twat."

"Oh, pooh."

She turned away, swirling the folds of the strange creation she wore. The dress had a high Victorian neck and billowy sleeves, which were suitable for a funeral mass. But the skirt split all the way up the middle, so Rosie's sequined bikini panties were visible.

"No way you are wearing that, babe," Rick said, pulling smartly at the brim of his straw hat.

"Rick." She twirled about again. "This is the newest thing in Soho. I'd wear tights, but it's too warm," she added, busily strapping on high-heeled satin sandals that focussed Rick's eyes on her gorgeous legs. She straightened up and he saw her sequined twat again.

"Nobody's got a right to see that. Only me," he protested.

"Honestly." She put her hands on her hips. "Sometimes I think you haven't changed at all. Sometimes I think you're like those other guys. Sometimes . . ."

"Forget it," he cut in abruptly. "Change your dress."

Ordinarily he wasn't macho, but the sight of Rosie's sequined bikini infuriated him. He'd given up rights to her twat for eight years while he was married to Sharon. During that time, Rosie experimented. But that was his fault, not hers. If he'd stayed where he truly belonged, no other man would have ever seen her sweet twat. Sometimes Rick woke up in the middle of the night in a sweat. In his dreams, a nameless, faceless man plunged into Rosie's private place. No, he vowed, no one else would ever see Rosie's twat again.

"Rick," she cajoled.

"Rosie. I mean it."

Rosie looked at Rick sadly. He was ruining her hopes for the male sex. She wanted men to be understanding so that women could be nicer. Whenever a man showed signs of being macho, Rosie made the assessment that women still had to be fierce.

"It's time to go," she hinted.

"Baby, you're not leaving here with that dress on."

"Compromise? Darling?"

"No way."

Suddenly, she was gone. When she returned, her legs

were covered. When the dress split open now, the black tights conveyed modesty. The look was also provocative, but Rick was modern and could handle that.

"Okay. Okay. You look great," he said, opening the elevator door.

"Bastard," she whispered. "I'm going to be hot all night because of your sexual insecurity."

"Shit." He reached for her.

"Don't touch me," she said defiantly. "If you're going to be like the rest of the guys on the street, I don't want to have anything to do with you."

She flounced her pretty head. Her hair was piled high in tiny spit curls, and Spanish combs held the delightful fluff in place. The hairstyle looked like cotton candy made in heaven. Rick followed Rosie into the car, pressed the lobby button, and when the car descended, took his hand away.

"What are you doing?"

"I'm isolating us."

"What for?"

"We're not going to leave this car until you melt down."

"We'll stay here forever."

"We'll miss Tatania's event."

"That crazy Hungarian can get along without us."

Rick knew Rosie wouldn't stay mad for long, so he simply pleaded with his eyes until she laughed and kissed him.

"Let's go," she said.

Though the gallery was only three blocks away, Rick did not want Rosie to walk down the street even with tights on. He hailed a cab. Three blocks passed swiftly. They exited at Prince Street and walked into the crowded gallery. Rick could see only outlines of large canvases because the crowd was blocking his view. The gallery was large, and cliques had formed. At Rick's left, poets huddled in a circle: poets without hair, poets with flowing hair, poets with exquisite tailoring, poets who looked like bums. And each and every poet had bad fingernails. Poets chewed fingernails down to the bone no matter how elegant they were. Quickly, Rick pushed past this corner. He hated chewed fingernails.

The next enclave was the politicos. They were a motley crew who smoked unfiltered cigarettes while organizing marches and rent strikes. This group looked like they had been given creamed spinach daily when they were young. Without them, SoHo would not have its useless struggle against the powerful real-estate lobby. Rick pulled Rosie away from this group just as quickly.

They walked toward the ovens, which reminded Rick of the Chinese women again. In front of the ovens were the artists. Rick could always tell painters because they dressed badly and had beautiful women hanging on their arms. These art groupies had always been enlisted from the nude models in art classes, but nowadays they were being infiltrated by the rock and film groupies. Rick zigzagged Rosie past the groupies, to four painters who stood apart from the others. In their center was Carlos, the star of the evening. The poor man looked done in. Tatania had dressed him in gold silk and the outfit was coming apart. Painters were like that. Even expensive clothing somehow fell apart on their bodies. Rick thought it must have something to do with their energy.

Rosie stopped short, wanting to congratulate Carlos. Unfortunately, Dalton Trimwell, the art critic for a SoHo paper, was talking to the group about Carlos's style.

"His gestural style is wonderful. One expects this from a Klein, but not from someone who is only thirty years old," Dalton was saying. Slim and tweedy, Dalton wore a film director's black leather jacket and white satin scarf, announcing to one and all that he was ready to direct a film.

"Yes," he continued, "there's a marvelous, passionate sense of combustion, exciting yet so self-contained." He turned his head, smiling approvingly at Rosie's dress. He frowned at Rick. Then back to Carlos. "Have you ever studied with the Maharishi?"

Carlos smiled benignly while sipping a tall rum punch and showing a number of blackened front teeth.

"You paint as if you want to ravish your model," Dalton analyzed.

"What model?" someone asked. "Carlos doesn't use a model."

Dalton's eyes twinkled. His slim nose shiveled up into a nervous tweak as he ushered his edict. "Ah, yes, he does. Even if it is only in his imagination. He has a model. Don't you?" He put his arm around the short Puerto Rican painter. "Don't you, Carlos?"

Carlos shrugged his shoulders.

"Like the green on that canvas. Look at it." Dalton pointed to a far corner.

"I'm hot in these tights," Rosie swore under her breath.

"Calm down. We'll say hello and split to a cool corner," Rick whispered back.

"That green," Dalton continued, hostile at the sound of their voices. "You must have taken that from somewhere."

"Seaweed," Carlos explained.

"Yes, theoretically seaweed can be a model."

"No, man, it's seaweed," Carlos said grimly, then caught sight of Rosie's skirt and smiled.

"Real seaweed?"

"Yeah, real seaweed," Carlos confirmed.

Annoyed, Dalton put a fresh gold-tipped cigarette into his Tiffany cigarette holder and chomped furiously on the stem.

Rosie took advantage of the momentary silence. "Congratulations," she said to Carlos. "I hope your show goes well. Have you met my husband?"

"I haven't met you, beautiful doll." Carlos rolled his eyes. His piercing black hair fell into curly bangs about his head, adding to his innocent pose.

"I thought you knew me. Tatania said you liked my book *Sweet Dreamdust*."

"You wrote that book?" Carlos became animated. He

shoved the rum punch into Dalton's sweaty palms and kissed Rosie on both cheeks. "What soul. What sex. What a babe."

"My husband, Rick," Rosie said again.

Carlos studied Rick's shoulders for a second, measuring them. Then he winked at Rosie as a conspirator might. Rosie unclamped Carlos's hands from her body as Dalton began to tell Carlos how his vision was like a jungle garden with high-tech inventiveness.

"Slob," Rosie said, as she and Rick headed off.

"He liked your book."

"I don't mean Carlos. After all, he's a painter and all painters are slobs. But Dalton. He sucks up to anyone who's making it."

"Is Carlos making it?"

"If Tatania has anything to say, he is."

"She is determined."

"Let's find her."

They walked through the crowd and finally spotted her, surrounded by several patrons wearing real jewels. Not all were women.

"Tatania," Rosie said, beaming.

"Darling. Have you met my Carlos? Did he tell you that he adores your book?" Tatania shimmered with joy.

"Hi," Rick said.

"Who loves you, baby?" She snuggled against Rick, putting husky arms about him, which squashed him. "Look at those canvases. Aren't they wonderful? Don't I know art? Huh?" She poked him and he doubled over.

"Tell you a secret." Tatania winked both dark eyes at once. "We're going to begin a new decade. Naturalistic art."

She turned, blowing kisses to her guests. She was wearing a flowing robe of red velvet, on which her personal seamstress had sewn sequined stars. With her natural grandiosity and her long hair braided and set up on her head like a crown, Tatania looked like royalty.

"You'll see," she whispered into Rosie's ear. "Carlos uses something real in every canvas. That's his secret."

"Seaweed," Rick commented.

"It's time. We're going to start," Tatania said.

"What's happening?" Rosie asked.

"We're going to unveil the *pièce de résistance*."

Like a beaver, Tatania cut a path through the mass of people. Rosie and Rick tried to follow but were left behind. In the center of the crowd, two assistants helped Tatania onto a pedestal where Carlos was nonchalantly picking at his teeth.

"This is a wonderful occasion for me and Carlos," Tatania announced while putting her huge arms around the man. Carlos grimaced, then, shrugging, conveyed that he was used to abuse and what of it.

"We are announcing the birth of a major movement in art. Naturalistic art. It comes from the Environmentalists and forms a third generation to the Abstract Expressionist Movement that put America on the map."

Tatania was as patriotic as only a Hungarian-born could be.

"Are you ready?" she asked the crowd.

"I'm going to the john," Rosie whispered. "I've got to take off these tights."

"Don't you dare," Rick warned, but she fled.

He stood there, furious at himself, knowing that the next time he saw her, the twat would be visible to the world. What was wrong with him? Couldn't he ever control Rosie? Maybe he should beat her. But the thought of harming one little hair of her adorable head turned his stomach. He watched for her reappearance. Then she was back, holding on to her split skirt modestly.

"I had to, Rick. I was suffocating. Besides, it's crowded. No one can see."

"Can't you put a safety pin there?" he asked, obsessed. Rosie shot him an annoyed look, then looked over his shoulder to where a canvas draped in silk caught her attention.

"The drape is coming down. Oh, Rick," she said, trying to get his attention away from her skirt.

Rick turned as the canvas was revealed to the crowd. Carlos's collage had cut-up drawings and lots of other things stuck on it.

"Is it real?" someone shouted.

"Yes," the crowd answered in a frenzy. The excitement caught and people pushed for a better look.

"It's a breakthrough!"

"Yes!"

"Wonderful!"

Rick spotted something odd.

"Rosie?"

"Yes, Rick. I see it."

Rick looked again, a wave of nausea coming over him.

"Don't faint," Rosie said.

But his stomach heaved and he leaned on her weakly. As she reached out to hold him, the skirt of her dress opened and her sequined bikini twat was visible. Rick aimed for it, snuggling against her as if holding on to dear life. No one else noticed Rosie's twat because they were concentrating on the left corner of Carlos's canvas. Leaning on Rosie, Rick looked at the canvas again. Yes, it was a dead hand. That made two.

It was midnight and the Alright Gallery was dark. Two men were on a ladder in front of Carlos's painting. Both were unshaven and wore dark hats.

"Think these frames are gold?"

"Naw. I wouldn't hang this in my house if they paid me a million smackeroos."

"But the boss wants it."

"Jeez, it's hard to get down."

"You've got to cut the damn thing."

"But . . . the boss said . . ."

"Hey, dope. Don't mention names."

"In here?"

"They got a speaker system. Who knows what else they got?"

"You want me to grab this end?"

"Maybe we can get it down if we both pull."

"Hey. Watch it."

"Those guards should be coming to."

"Those Chinks are something. Did you see the way they tried to chop us down?"

"It's karate and they're not Chinks."

"They look like Chinks."

"Stupid, Chinks don't have kinky hair."

"They don't?"

"Stop bullshitting and grab this."

"Maybe we should try to get the hand down."

"Yeah, let's leave the stupid picture there."

"Hey, that's a good idea."

"Maybe we should check with the boss first."

"They musta used some kind of glue."

"Maybe we should use a saw."

"You got a saw?"

"Let's look in the back."

With no warning, the ladder slipped. Louie the Lip and Aldo the Arm came crashing down.

Bammmm. Wahooomm. Grunt.

The canvas fell onto the shiny oak floor. Then it twisted and little bits fell from it. Seashells. Horse hair. But the hand stayed on.

"Damned hand."

"Hey, someone's coming."

"I found a saw."

"It's gonna make a ton of noise."

"So what. It's night."

"Hey, that big dame who owns the place is coming in the door."

"So let's get her."

Louie grabbed a rope and tossed it to Aldo.

As Tatania walked into the gallery, the beasts pulled the rope. She fell, causing an immense bang on the floorboards. The beasts relaxed. But Tatania screamed. The men panicked and ran out to the curb, where a car waited. Soon they were speeding toward the Holland Tunnel.

"I got a bad feeling this isn't the end of those damn hands," Louie said grimly to his pals.

11

The next morning, Tatania reported the severed hand to the police. Several days flew by as the entire issue became more and more complex. The police refused to give up the two dead hands, because they were evidence in a murder case. The Salernos requested the hands, because they could not bury Mr. and Mrs. Salerno in sacred ground without them. Rick found out why. It was a custom in their native town of Venviento, Sicily, that a body be buried whole or the deceased soul would be in limbo forever. This Sicilian custom was not endorsed by the Pope, whose only concern was that the dead be given the last rites and be buried in hallowed ground. In Sicily, each township interpreted the Roman edicts in its own way. So the Salernos waited at the Fierello Mortuary while the family tried to impress upon the authorities that the funeral wake and service could not be performed without the dead hands.

The media became interested. CBS sent two crews down to interview Tatania Sirlanki and Carlos about the hand in his canvas. Carlos was formally charged with withholding evidence, though he explained calmly that he had found the hand on Spring Street the afternoon of the opening, and had thought: *What luck; I can make an important statement about naturalistic art with a real hand.* Tatania hired the finest public-relations representation for Carlos and the press crowded into the gallery to see the vacant spot on Carlos's canvas where the hand had been.

It seemed that everyone wanted the hands. But not Rick. Unfortunately, he began dreaming about the hands. Two hands in prayer. In a wedding ceremony. On dead corpses. He'd wake up screaming, sweaty, and Rosie would put her arms around him and say, "Silly. They're only hands." Rick hadn't been able to accept the fact that he became hysterical whenever he thought of the two severed hands, while Rosie remained calm.

Rosie was working efficiently, taping everything. She managed to get several important interviews for the book. Tatania spoke to her. So did Carlos. So did the Salerno sister-in-law, who called the police bloody murderers. Rosie went to local clubs where ordinary persons would not be allowed entrance, and asked the *paisanos* about Venviento's custom. Where did the custom that a dead person could not be buried without their limbs originate? Suppose someone had an accident and lost a foot? Did that mean they were forever cursed? Yes, the old men nodded. That's why Venviento had lost all of its young people. No one wanted to live in a place like that. Especially since Venviento was in the center of the accursed Black Hand organization and men were always losing parts of their bodies, the organization taking a special delight in punishing detractors in this very personal way.

Rosie's tape collection grew. She went to the Italian consulate on Park Avenue, asked to see the cultural attaché, and spoke to him about the Venviento custom of burial. The fancy man was embarrassed. He claimed not to know about this strange Sicilian custom. The consulate did not like to convey to the American press that Italians were primitive, superstitious peasants.

All the while Rosie taped, Rick stayed home and worried. Rosie persevered and had the book outline ready, which would command a financial advance. She'd finished the preliminary research and written the first two drafts of the outline. Then she handed it to Rick, who polished, rewrote, and inserted a non-Italian objective viewpoint. He read it over carefully. It was good. Rosie was putting her heart and soul into it. Her outline on the severed hands chapter was extraordinary. How could she do it? But there it was. A blow-by-blow description of how Rick had found the severed hand, how she'd returned to take photos, how the cops and Kushel had entered the picture. Then the other hand, discovered on Carlos's canvas, how she and Rick had gone home and said nothing to Tatania, how some beasts had tried to steal the hand from the canvas, and how the cops had finally arrived and claimed the hand for evidence. She'd written in all the blood, the gore, the mangled hands. How could Rosie handle this?

Rick put the outline down and joined Rosie, who was in the bathtub. She was immersed in wonderful perfumed bubbles, her dark hair tied high with pink satin ribbons. She smiled at Rick. Without a word, he dropped his sweatsuit, looked down at his erection, looked up at Rosie, and winked, then joined her in the tub. Quietly they sat there, looking at each other. Her smile was contagious and soon he was relaxing, his lids heavy.

"You look sexy," she whispered, then lay beside him in the tub. Slowly, she began to caress him. His heart fluttered. He was lucky. Everyone said that only Japanese women did this kind of thing. But not so. Rosie did everything. She'd read all the books on Tantric and Taoist sex and knew techniques like the butterfly lick. Rosie believed that men loved to be caressed and fondled and kissed and that women did all of that best. Rosie guided him into her, conveying with her body what her lips had never revealed, that he was part of her. He sighed, content, exploring the inner sweetness of this wanton woman he'd had the good fortune to marry.

Afterwards, she lay on top of Rick, her head on his chest, soapy curls brushing his eyes whenever she moved.

She looked up at him happily. "Hi," she whispered.

"Rosie . . ." he began. But he knew better than to ask an Italian a direct question. Based on his personal experience with Rosie and with the community at large, Italians always shot a hostile look at any question no matter what it was.

What time is it?

What day is it?

What town is it?

Perfectly ordinary questions, but to Italians, questions to ponder.

What would Rosie say to his question?

"Rosie, darling, how can you deal with the hands?" he blurted.

There it was. Now he waited for the explosion. But he was lucky. Rosie was feeling intimate. Sex was the natural binder of souls. She looked sad for a moment, then shrugged her soapy shoulders in a gesture of hopelessness.

"You don't know?"

"No," Rick said. "I don't. And I don't understand how you could . . ."

She shot him one of her "Oh, my God, you're hopeless" looks. Then she said, "It was the way I was brought up."

"But I know how you were brought up. Remember, I was around then. Your father protected you from everything and everybody, even your own mother."

"That's not exactly what I mean."

"Would you explain, please?"

"It has nothing to do with us. I mean, my family. It's those beasts."

"Go on."

She hesitated. Then she took a sponge bought in Mexico when she was still single and dating other men. He hated the sponge. She dipped it into the soapy water and began scrubbing Rick's skin. The sponge was known to peel off the top layer of body skin which experts say ages first. Rick relaxed, enjoying her touch.

"It's the beasts. Every once in a while they would take to the streets."

"Take to the streets?"

"It would be *High Noon* in SoHo. All the families would

stay home, doors shut. No one would go out even if they ran out of milk for the baby. And it wouldn't matter if they did, because the grocery stores were closed. The postman would not deliver mail. Old people would be taken for visits to their families in suburbia when it happened."

"When what happened?"

"*High Noon.*"

"What the hell is *High Noon?*"

"Ricky, you've seen the movie. It was like that."

"A gunfight?"

"More than that. The beasts are more imaginative. Remember, they're descendants of the Romans."

Rosie loved the Roman Empire passionately. Whenever they spoke of sexual fantasies, Rosie's were always of Roman orgies, Roman villas, Roman grapes, Roman wine, and Roman gladiators. She felt that the Romans were the last of the supreme organizers; she admired their discipline and their *mano a mano* stance in the Colosseum.

"So they fought in an arena?" Rick asked, puzzled.

"Yup. In SoHo that meant the streets. I think that's why the artists were attracted to the place."

"Huh?"

Her logic was losing him, but her sponging was exciting.

"No. Let me finish explaining," she said when he caressed her.

"So . . ."

"You see," she continued, "I believe the artists came to SoHo because of all the bloodshed here."

"Artists came here because it was cheap."

"That's what they say, but think about my theory."

Rick thought about it and didn't agree. But he held back his opinion because he wanted to hear all about *High Noon.*

"*High Noon?*" he hinted.

"Well, Rick, you see . . ." She hesitated then. "I saw *High Noon* once."

He sat up, rigid. "No!"

"Yes. That's where it happened."

"What happened?"

She sighed. Then she rinsed out the soapy sponge, wrung it dry, and threw it into the tub water again, where it floated.

"Dad had taken me to Poughkeepsie to visit my aunt. Mom had the flu and couldn't come. It was a wedding or something important and that branch of the family was dying to see me, so they convinced Dad to come without Mom. You know he never did that." Rick nodded. "We came back the next day. It was sunny, so when we left the railroad we decided to take the Fifth Avenue bus downtown. We had fun. Dad knew that Mom was feeling better because she'd called early that morning. So we took our time. We rode down to Washington Square Park and for some reason decided to walk down West Broadway. It was very quiet on West Broadway. The area wasn't SoHo yet.

"Dad noticed it was too quiet. He became nervous. Then he saw that the luncheonette on the corner of Houston and West Broadway was shut tight. He looked over to the grocery store in the middle of the next block. It wasn't open either. And there were no cars on the street. Dad got very pale, grabbed me up into his arms, and ran fast. We were lucky. One of the doors in an industrial building was ajar. Dad shoved me inside. We got behind the doors just in time."

"In time for what?"

"Here. You take the sponge," she said, handing it to Rick.

"I'll soap you down," he volunteered.

She turned and he began sponging her body with the soapy stuff. She was tense all over. Her neck muscles were tight, her back was locked. Rick swore as he kneaded her body, but the rigidity would not bend.

"Maybe you don't want to go on," Rick said, worrying.

"No. You said you wanted to understand. So do you want me to tell you everything?"

"Yes."

"We heard a screech of cars coming to a stop. Dad was holding me up to his chest, and we could look out the tiny glass square in the door. There were two black cars. I knew something terrible was happening because my father began to tremble. He had never done that before, not even when Grandpa died. He put my head down on his lapel so I couldn't see, but I struggled. I was always my own girl." She laughed softly. "Then I saw them."

"Who?"

"Lots of men in dark suits and dark hats getting out of the cars. They were dressed like movie stars, only they hadn't shaved. I didn't know who they were, but they all looked familiar. I had seen them before, walking down the streets or hanging out in cafés. I don't know. But I remember there were a lot of them and they were holding on to one man. He'd been tortured or something. On his forehead was a long cut, and his chest was covered with blood. They'd torn most of his clothes off, but his pants were still on. Then I saw they had cut his tongue off. He was a mess."

Rick was feeling queasy.

"You all right?" she asked.

"Yes."

"They hadn't finished with him. They tied him to a lamppost with a heavy cord. Round and round, like a western movie with Indians. I began to cry, but Dad put his hand over my mouth. I struggled. I couldn't breathe. But I knew I had to keep perfectly still. I was only six years old and knew that something awful could happen to us."

"Six? Jesus. Baby."

He put his wet arms about her and held her tightly to his chest. She was trembling. He kissed her gently, noticing that her eyes were moist with tears.

"Then they did it."

"What more could they do?" Rick said in anguish.

"One man had a cleaver, the kind that old butcher shops have." Rick nodded. "Anyhow, he tore off the man's pants and chopped off his penis. The man was still alive because he screamed. I'll always remember that bloody scream."

She shook her head, then put it on his shoulder and began crying soft, sad tears for the man she didn't know who had died so long ago.

"He died soon after," she continued after her sobbing had stopped. "They got into the cars and tore off again. Dad was shaking. I began crying and he hummed an Italian lullaby he used to sing to me when I was a baby. We waited. I was hungry. I wet my pants. I wanted to go home. Dad waited until he was sure the cars had gone. Then we ran out. Dad was holding me tight, and we ran down the block, up Prince Street, and reached home. When we walked into our apartment, we heard the police sirens. I remember how glad I was to see Mom. She was yelling and screaming. The entire family was in our apartment. Dad had two drinks fast. Then he changed his clothes. He had peed in his pants, too. Then Mom undressed me, cleaned me up, and gave me food. Then Dad took me on his lap and told me to forget what I had seen. It was only a bad dream, he said. I said I would. He knew I never would."

"And you never have."

"Nope," she whispered. "I've never forgotten what the beasts did to that poor man."

"Why did they do it?"

"People said he had talked. That's the way they fix people who talk. Or used to."

"They?"

"I had bad dreams about them for years afterwards. Dad told me to forget. He said he would always take care of me. And he always did."

"Now I understand why he's upset about the book."

"Yes. He thinks they might give us trouble."

"Do you think they will?"

She looked different now. Fierce. "Let them."

"Do you still think about that day?" he asked gently.

She relaxed. "Yes. But I think that day was the reason I fell in love with you."

"Huh?"

"Yes, really."

"I thought it was the skateboard."

"It was, kind of. You were strong. My God, you've always had those muscles." She playfully squeezed his shoulders. "But you never used them. Instead, you were sweet and dear. Like Dad is. I fell in love with you because of the way you are. Besides, you weren't Italian. I could never fall in love with an Italian."

"But your Dad is one."

"But he's my Dad, and besides, he's special."

"Not all Italian men are like them."

"Maybe. But I could never take the chance."

Something dawned on Rick. "Rosie, why do you laugh at *The Godfather*? Is there a connection?"

They'd seen the film twenty-seven times, and each time she laughed hysterically through the gory scenes.

"Yes, there is."

"I don't understand. What?"

"Ricky, if I didn't laugh, I would have cried."

"But why didn't you tell me this before."

"I couldn't."

"Why not?"

"Because I didn't trust you."

"And you trust me now."

Her eyes grew mysterious.

"Rosie," he began, "we've known each other since we were kids, for God's sake. We live together. We married in church," he added to impress her. "And you still don't trust me."

"No, Rick. Not entirely."

"Why not?"

"You should know why not."

"No, I don't."

She pulled back from him. The bubble bath was beginning to lose its mist and he could see her body clearly through the water.

She paused, then said, "Because of Sharon."

His heart fell. She was still throwing Sharon up to him.

"Rosie. Can't you forget that?"

"No. I can't. You see, when you left me for Sharon, you proved they were right."

"Who's they?"

"The people I grew up with. They say you can never trust someone who isn't Italian. I did. Dad did, too. We both loved you from the first minute we saw you, didn't we?"

"Yes, you did."

"And we treated you like one of the family even though you had that crazy father and mother, didn't we?"

He remembered the long Sunday dinners with cousins, aunts, uncles, and Mario holding forth with the folk stories he loved to tell.

"Yes, you did," he agreed nostalgically.

"That's why the thing with Sharon meant so much," she said simply. "Because you betrayed me. And once betrayed, we never forgive."

"But you did forgive me. You married me." Her tears tasted salty as Rick kissed her cheeks.

"Yes, I did."

"So you went against them."

"Yes."

"Why?"

"Because I love you."

12

After that, Rick felt that he had to come through for Rosie. When she asked him to attend the Salerno funeral wake, though he had no desire to view the deceased sans hands, he agreed to go. The law had intervened and forced the burial because of the health code. The community grumbled, but there was nothing anyone could do. SoHo was not Sicily, though many had not yet given up that fantasy. The community considered boycotting the wake, but natural compassion for the bereaved overcame their fury at the officials, and most decided to attend.

This Italian fury toward American law had its roots in the fact that America was not Italy. Even as they enjoyed the opportunities that this country offered, Italians pretended that they were still living in Italy. That's why they set up enclaves where they could exist separately. They were ill at ease, and the special customs and rituals comforted them. This separatism worked both for and against them. It was a political liability; since they couldn't agree on any issue, they had no clout. But it was also an advantage. It allowed them to be the rebellious eccentrics they are naturally. Because, as George Orwell had predicted, everything American had become a fusion of cardboard and computer copies, the Italians were off-beat.

At the funeral parlor, Rick thought everyone looked like part of a Puccini opera. Rick felt he, himself, looked like an extra.

"Wear black," Rosie had ordered.

"Don't have anything black. I'm not into S&M," he joked.

"Wear gray."

They were both dressed in dark gray for the funeral wake. The place was elegant, with marble pillars, soft green couches, and plenty of palm trees. Real palm trees. The men sat in the lobby, in one group, smoking cigars, telling lewd stories while wearing official black. The women huddled in another group, swapping sexual gossip and recipes. At the left of the lobby was the entrance to the inner sanctum, where the Salerno corpses lay underneath two ruffled satin coverlets with a white pearl rosary sewn on each one. Her coverlet was white. His was gray.

As the guests entered, everyone stared. Rick and Rosie were no exception. They walked through the lobby as strangers greeted them.

"I'm Mrs. Adamo from down the street. You remember me, no?" a fat woman asked them.

"I'm Mr. Caputo, the butcher," an elderly man said as he shook Rick's hands with great emphasis.

Rick smiled at the well-wishers from the SoHo community. He did not recognize any faces, for today they were somber citizens greeting one another affectionately while viewing death on its own formal terms.

"How's your father?" a thin woman asked Rosie.

"Fine," Rosie answered. "Come on, dear," she said, leading Rick into the inner sanctum, adding, "please don't up-chuck or do anything sloppy."

"I've turned over a new leaf."

"What's that?"

"I'm going to be your knight in shining armor."

They walked toward the coffin and knelt at a pew. Rick wasn't Catholic, but he bowed his head anyway.

"Don't boast about it," Rosie whispered, seemingly deep in prayer.

"About what?"

"About being a hero. Just do it."

"Okay," he answered, sure of himself.

Then he saw them.

Rosie was right. Sally Salerno had been beautiful. Her hair was like black velvet. Her skin was translucent white, and the cosmetician had performed well on her dark lashes and red lips. Her body was slim and dressed in a red velvet gown, cut off at the halfway point by the coffin. Rick didn't want to think about the hidden part of Sally.

In contrast, Tony Salerno was pudgy. His head was square, he had bushy eyebrows, and he wore a sweet smile. Poor bastard, Rick thought. He turned away and tried not to think of Tony's hand either.

They walked to the first row of relatives. There were twenty rows of chairs. Rick felt claustrophobic. How many Italians could one family know? He held his breath, vowing not to embarrass the Caesare clan by ignoring custom. So he dutifully followed Rosie as she introduced herself to an entire row of people, saying, "I'm Mario Caesare's daughter. And this is my husband, Rick." When she nodded to the others seated in endless rows of chairs, he did too. Then she talked to an old woman sitting close to Anita Salerno, the late Tony Salerno's sister-in-law. Rick waited. Finally, Rosie joined him and they walked to the rear of the large room. When they sat on a small couch, many eyes were watching.

Rick knew that Rosie had both a tape recorder and a camera in her safari bag. As a good reporter, she took them along, just in case.

"I could get a great shot of the corpses from here," she noted.

"Mario would kill you."

She grimaced.

A wild vibration began to surge through the room. Everyone's attention turned from Rick and Rosie to someone in the doorway. Strange expectant looks appeared on mourners' faces. Four men walked in. They were tall and muscular, and formed a cordon around two shorter men. These two walked in and looked around. Then they signaled the others, who took positions about the room. The two short men waited, each beside a coffin.

"What's going on?" Rick asked.

"Shhh," Rosie warned. "And whatever you do, don't get up." Rick watched as everyone in the room rose. He thought of the Metropolitan Opera when the audience stands and cheers the performers. He'd been present when this had happened and it was exhilarating. The room had that same sense of excitement, only without applause.

A tall, slim man walked into the room, discreetly lifted his hand, and everyone resumed sitting. He walked toward the coffins, where he did not kneel but simply bent his head in reverence. Then he turned, flanked by the two short men, and greeted the family. Rick examined him closely. Was he one of the beasts? If he was, he didn't look like anyone from the Coppola movie. Instead, he looked like Paul Newman. His body moved quickly and with grace. His cold eyes darted about the room and flickered on Rosie and Rick too long. Under her breath, Rosie swore.

"Damn," she said.

"Don't worry, I'm here."

"Rick, you don't know."

The man began to walk toward the rear of the room, looking at them. Rick began to shiver. Would he be murdered in front of all these people?

Everyone watched as the man turned toward them. But when Mario and Celia suddenly appeared, he hesitated. They did not walk toward the coffins. Instead, they joined Rosie and Rick at the couch. The man stopped. Then he turned, and joined Anita Salerno again. There was much weeping as several older women wailed and beat their breasts harshly.

"You should have waited for us," Mario scolded Rick.

"Rosie didn't say anything."

"You've been in this family a long time, kid. You should know these things."

Rick nodded. Mario was right. He should think Italian.

"Listen. Why don't we have lunch this week. I'll explain things to you. My daughter won't listen. She's hard-headed."

Celia nodded in agreement while Rosie glared at Rick.

"Don't think so," Rick said.

"I'm on your side, Ricky."

"I've got to be careful, Mario."

"We've all got to be careful. That's my point."

More people entered the room. They were all watching the man who looked like Paul Newman. Finally, the bleating women quieted down. Then Anita Salerno whispered into the slim man's ear. Listening, he kept nodding, apparently promising Anita something.

"Why are they friendly?" Rick asked.

"Not now," his wife answered.

"I don't understand. If he's one of the beasts, then why is the family being nice to him?"

"Because they don't blame him," she explained.

Mario grunted in agreement.

"Whom do they blame then?" Rick continued.

"Sally."

"Sally? But she's the victim."

"Yes, but they feel if she hadn't been fooling around, none of this would have happened."

"That's not fair."

"You're getting the message."

For the first time, Rick understood Rosie's bitter feminism.

The man snapped his fingers and the guard of honor encircled him. As he exited, people bowed with respect. Still mesmerized, Rick watched as Rosie disappeared into the crowd until he could no longer see her.

"Going to the men's room," he said to his in-laws.

Inside the men's bathroom, Rick's nerves gave and he had an attack of diarrhea. How did these Italians handle all this drama, he thought. Was it something in the pasta?

Two men walked in. He listened as they used the urinals. Then they spoke.

"My God, Vito coming here."

"He always had a lot of guts."

As Rick departed from the enclosed toilet, they were struck deaf and dumb. Rick saw that one was Joe, the tailor on Prince Street, and the other was the man who owned the bread store on Bleecker Street, whose name Rick could never remember.

He nodded curtly as they eyed him with hostility.

Outside, everything was in confusion. It took him a while to spot Rosie. Finally, he found her talking to a frail old woman.

"Rosie, where have you been?"

"Do you remember Lucia?" She motioned to the woman. "She was at our wedding. She was the midwife who delivered me."

Rosie always boasted about the fact that she was born au naturel in her mother's bed. She preferred Mario's version of the story. He said she was born as the sun rose and he held her up to Father Sun, dedicating her to him. Celia remembered Rosie's birth to be in the dead of night. Rosie offered these two versions as examples of the differences in her parents' perspectives.

"Hello," Rick said to the woman.

When she smiled, wrinkles took over her face.

"It's not too bad being old," she laughed. As she spoke, Rick saw that she had all her teeth. "They're real." She pointed to them with pride. "Everything is real. I've never had one organ removed. I'm like a newborn baby."

"Lucia, *grazie*." Rosie kissed the woman's wrinkled forehead. "May we walk you home?"

"I like to walk too slow for young people." She crackled with laughter and her eyes lit up like a lighthouse beacon as she walked away.

"Rosie, come home," Mario urged when he finally found them.

It was a command, so they followed Mario and Celia down Sullivan Street and around to Thompson, where the Caesare apartment was located. As soon as they were there, Celia put her apron on and began warming up the food she'd prepared earlier in the day. Sausage and peppers. Calzone. Ricotta with shells. Chicken with mushrooms. Veal with wine. Whenever Celia put a plate on the table, she gave Rosie a harsh look for not helping her. Rosie ignored her mother. Instead, she watched her father pouring wine into glasses.

"What I don't get is how those damn hands traveled," Mario said. He offered them a glass of wine, but they refused.

"Got any ideas?" Rosie asked.

"This isn't for your book," he said. "I'd just like to know."

He scratched his forehead, trying to revive his thinking tools, and sipped the wine, looking at it carefully as if the glass could reveal the answer to his query.

"I've got to go to the john." Rosie lugged her safari bag into the bathroom.

"She's a good girl," Mario said earnestly after she left. "But stubborn."

"Like all the Caesare women," Celia snipped.

Mario gestured with his arms. "She can't help it. It's in her blood."

"Rosie's great," Rick defended.

"You"—Celia waved her arms at him—"you should stop her. You're her husband."

"We don't have that kind of relationship."

"What relationship? Marriage is marriage," Celia insisted. "Eat." She pointed to the food.

"Later," Mario replied. "Sit down." Celia sat next to him, looking completely resigned. Rick thought that his mother-in-law was odd. She was always sweet and calm except when talking about her daughter.

"What's she doing in the bathroom?" Mario asked.

"Maybe she's pregnant." Celia looked hopeful.

"We're not going to have children," Rick announced.

Mario's eyes bulged. "You're going to deprive me of grandchildren," he said in anguish.

"Can we get back to the hands?" Rick asked.

"No grandchildren. What's wrong with you? Don't you like kids?" Mario asked.

"Rosie doesn't want them."

Desperately, Celia threw up her hands, looking up at the ceiling. "What woman wants kids?"

"You did," her husband said.

"I should have had five more. Then my heart wouldn't be broken."

"Broken?" Rick repeated.

"She's broken my heart. We spoiled her."

"She's not spoiled," Rick defended. "She's different."

"But why does she have to be different?" Celia anguished.

"She's a writer," Rick said. "Now, what about the hands?"

Mario sipped his wine. "That Vito. He doesn't come to everyone's funeral. He must have really loved Sally."

"Is he from SoHo?"

Violently, Mario shook his head.

"He lives in Jersey. He's got thirty-six rooms. He's the only Italian who has a room for all of his relatives." Mario laughed gustily. Then he soured. "That beast."

"Shh," Celia warned, looking out the windows for eavesdroppers.

"Is he a . . ." Rick couldn't say it.

"He's a beast." Then Mario shouted, "Hey, Rosie, what are you doing in there anyhow?"

"Mario? The hands? How did one get to Mercer Street and the other to Spring Street?"

The older man shrugged his shoulders. "Magic," he answered.

Rosie reappeared, looking excited. "Rick, we've got to go."

"You haven't eaten a thing," her mother complained.

"We're slimming." She tugged at Rick's sleeve. "Come on, darling."

"Rosie? Are you doing anything you shouldn't?" Her father was suspicious.

"No, Pop."

Mario's cheeks bulged with fury. His glass of wine was on the table before him and it spilled when he banged his fist on the table.

"Never call me Pop," he ordered.

Rosie blew a kiss to her parents while Celia examined her. "That skirt is too short. The slit is too high. Those shoes are too open. Your hair is too wild," she admonished her daughter.

"See you," Rosie said.

"Was your mother always like that?" Rick asked when they were on the street.

"Not at first."

"When did it start?"

"When Dad and I shut her out. I can't blame her. It's not easy being the odd person when two people adore each other."

"Don't know how that feels."

"It feels like . . ." Then she bit her lip. Rick knew that she was thinking about him and Sharon. He grabbed her hand and squeezed it tightly.

"When I married you, I thought she'd let up. But she didn't. She said you were too handsome to marry."

"Am I?" he laughed.

"I'm not sure."

They stopped in the doorway of a chic boutique while Rosie kissed Rick. Suddenly, the store dummy in the window moved and Rick jumped.

"Silly. That's a real woman."

"No?"

He watched as the gaunt woman moved as a dummy would, and was surprised when she winked at him.

"Fabulous," Rick said. "SoHo is a great place to live."

"Come on, handsome," Rosie said jealously.

They walked up West Broadway. People sat in outdoor cafés watching the world go by. SoHo was as close to Paris as one could want.

Rosie began walking faster.

"Why are we rushing, darling?"

"Because I have a surprise."

Her mood was high when they reached home. "I couldn't wait to tell you," she said, reaching into her safari bag.

"Tell me what?"

"Lucia taped the whole conversation when the beast was talking to Anita Salerno. Wait till you hear it!"

"So that's what you were doing in the bathroom?"

She laughed.

"But Lucia? Isn't it dangerous?"

"She says she's too old to worry about death."

Rosie pressed the button down on the tape recorder. There was a lot of background garble and Rick couldn't distinguish anything.

"This is it," she said.

"Is there anything I can do for the family?" the voice on the tape said.

"That's the beast," Rosie explained.

"We need those hands, Don Vito," another voice said.

"That's Anita Salerno."

The tape garbled. Someone said the deceased looked beautiful. Someone else said it was good that the Salerno daughter was not allowed at the wake. Someone said the flowers were beautiful. Someone said it was terribly crowded.

"Here it comes," Rosie said.

Clear and true, the beast's voice was heard.

"Don't worry about it. We'll get the hands back. Count on it."

13

"Got time for a bite, kid?" Mario sounded hassled on the phone.

"Got to check with Rosie," Rick said.

"Don't you do anything without her?"

"Can I call you?"

"Naw. Meet me at the Elengo Taverno at five-thirty."

The phone clicked. Mario never took no for an answer. Rick went into the kitchen. The refrigerator was stocked with two-liter bottles of Coke, Rosie's stash. On the second shelf were cans of Coke, which Rick was permitted to use only if there was absolutely nothing else in the house he could drink. He looked around. He did not feel like apple juice. Besides, the juice looked yellow and smelled bad. He grabbed a can of Coke from Rosie's stash, opened it, and jogged down to the couch, where he sat, patting his stomach while he downed the Coke.

He closed his eyes, listening to the soft ticking of Rosie's typewriter in the study, a corner of the bedroom that she had roped off. Rick could never go into the bedroom while work progressed.

"Rosie?" He disobeyed the severe rule of never interrupting her creative flow. Rosie clicked on, hard at work, making their fortune.

"Rick? You busy?" Arnoldo hissed from inside the elevator car, sounding like a snake. Rick walked to the elevator, unlocked the door, and saw his neighbor hunched in a corner.

"What's up?"

"Do you have a minute?" Arnoldo's eyes popped as he focussed, conveying fear at the possibility of Rosie's presence.

"Can you come up to my loft?" he asked Rick.

"What for?"

"I have something to show you."

Rick searched for a reason to say no. When he couldn't think of one, he stepped into the elevator car, which began without human touch.

"The computer is on energy transport," Arnoldo explained.

"Don't let Rosie catch you."

Arnoldo's eyes burned with paranoia. "Everybody's scared of her."

"She's nice."

Arnoldo hung his head and looked like the thin circus clown who entertained on stilts. When the elevator reached the top floor, he put one foot gingerly in front of the other, creeping quietly into the loft.

"Listen," he said to Rick.

Rick heard a soft motor humming like the ignition of an expensive Bentley. Then, something metal moved.

"What the hell?"

"It's the Princess," Arnoldo explained.

Before them stood a metal robot, very square with long, thick prongs for arms and a thin, pointed head.

"Isn't she wonderful?" Arnoldo whispered. "She's a sensor robot that calculates ambient temperature. I invented her."

"What for?"

"You'll see. Princess, would you get Mr. Ramsey a martini?"

"I don't drink," Rick cautioned.

"She doesn't know that. Anyhow, when did you stop drinking?"

"When I found the hand."

"What hand?"

The robot walked to the refrigerator, opened the door, and took out an ice tray, which it emptied out into a cocktail shaker. Then, using both metal arms, it picked up bottles of gin and dry vermouth at once, filling the shaker with exactly the right amounts, lifted a long spoon, and stirred.

"Makes a great martini," Arnoldo observed.

"What else does it do?"

"She," Arnoldo corrected. "White wine on the rocks for me, Princess," he ordered.

As the robot obeyed, there was a faint odor of gas.

"She's leaking," Rick observed.

"Damn," Arnoldo cursed. "Got to fix her."

He walked over to the robot, who had finished bartending and was waiting for the next command. Arnoldo took a long screwdriver from his pocket. Then Rick heard harsh churning sounds, and some squeaks.

"There. All fixed. Go to it, Princess."

The robot glided over to the sofa, its prongs carrying the drinks. Arnoldo collected them and put them on the table.

"Great!" He patted the mechanical object. "She's wonderful, isn't she, Rick? She's an experimental prototype equipped with a range of sensors that respond to verbal commands. She moves forward and backward, raises or lowers either arm, and grips and releases objects, including the human hand. Rick, give her your hand."

"Don't think so."

"Go on."

Rick put out his hand. When the Princess touched his flesh, he squealed, "She's cold!"

"Don't say that too loud."

"Don't let my wife see this thing."

"Why not?"

"Rosie has a theory that modern man is planning to eliminate the need for human woman."

"That's paranoid."

"Is it?"

"Henpecked, aren't you?"

"That's enough, old chap," Rick said crisply.

Arnoldo turned to the Princess. "She's much superior to a human woman," he said proudly.

"Doesn't look like that adorable robot in *Star Wars*," Rick said nastily.

At the mention of this, the robot went into a frenzy. Zzzhuuuuuu. Brrrhrrrrr. Chugggguggh.

"You've upset the Princess," Arnoldo admonished Rick.

"Later."

Rick walked into the elevator and pressed the button for his floor. As the doors shut, he saw Arnoldo trying to pacify his beloved. Maybe the Princess was why Arnoldo never dated.

"Rick? Where have you been?" Rosie called as he entered their loft.

"Finished?"

"We've got a meeting with the movie people. Get out of your sweatsuit."

"Honey, you look fabulous."

She glowed at his compliment. She was dressed in a long white silk jacket, which crossed under the breast and complimented its matching pleated skirt. Around her neck were the soft white pearls he'd given her when she was seventeen. Her hair was drawn back severely, but a large white bowler hat hid most of it.

"You're charm, poetry, excess, extravagance, and elegance, all in one," he said softly.

"More gloss?"

"No. You look perfect."

"More junk?"

"Nope."

The junk referred to Rosie's personal stash of jewelry, which filled enormous baskets. She called it her Ali Baba junk. She had brooches from another century, rhinestone crosses, hearts painted in Italy, and other strange finds. Rosie said that having this treasure made her feel as if she were living in the Casbah illegally.

"Wear your linen suit," she said. "Those guys from Hollywood like white linen suits."

"But I've got to meet Mario."

"How come?"

"Don't know."

"Well, this is only a hello meeting."

"You can handle that."

"Meet you here later?"

"Right."

She picked up a large white bag. "Oh," she said quickly, "if you're meeting Dad, wear your dark brown suit."

"Why that one?"

She laughed. "It makes you look Italian."

"Hey, you look good, Ricky," Mario led Rick through the quaint Thompson Street restaurant to a corner table. The restaurant was empty except for one couple. Rick recognized the man as Fast Bob Talbot, a West Coast literary agent with small feet and large ears. Fast Bob was necking with a young blonde. Rick's eyes wandered about the place. It was a modest restaurant with immaculate tablecloths. On the walls were paintings of Capri and the Bay of Naples. The renderings were very bad. Italians never hung pictures of the Romans or Leonardo. Instead, their restaurants always proudly displayed bad art. In SoHo, everyone said that if the walls had awful paintings, the food had to be good.

"Calamari?" Mario ordered as the waiter attended them. "Linguini fini?"

"Vegetables," Rick said. "I'm on a diet."

"Give him escarole with garlic. And some zucchini friti."

The waiter shook his head as he walked off. Vegetarians were not popular in Italian restaurants, though Italians, like the Chinese, were excellent chefs of the leaf.

"Hi, Mario," the bartender waved. He was a huge man with a curly mustache, who looked like an extra from the Grand Ole Opry.

"Tim's an actor," Mario explained. "You've seen him on those beer commercials."

He was silent as he poured wine from the bottle.

"That's disgusting," he said, as Fast Bob's tongue visibly entered the girl's mouth. "She's young enough to be his daughter."

"Doesn't look too sanitary."

"Sex is great. It's the spice of life. But sex with a child is sick."

"Seems to be popular."

"But that don't make it right." Mario sipped his wine. "The thing is, kid, that this country is on its way down the tubes. Like the Romans. Did they stop fooling around with those orgies when the Empire was falling apart? No. See what happened? That's where America is going. This thing with sex and children? Even the beasts don't do that."

"Not yet."

Mario's eyes grew harsh. "Guess you're right. When they begin killing women, there's no telling what they'll do next."

He shook his head as Rick shot a sneaky look at Fast Bob playing fast and loose.

"You're a nice kid, Ricky. You're good to my daughter. Except for that Sharon thing. You broke her heart then. She went crazy."

"I was wrong."

The bartender picked up a banjo and strummed away, singing a Neopolitan love song. Mario glanced at him.

"Mario. I have something important to ask."

"So ask."

"Do you think we're courting trouble?"

"That's why I wanted to see you. So far, I have protected you. I know some things and the beasts know I know them. But if you get out of hand with this book"—he threw his hands up in the air in a hopeless gesture—"who knows what will happen?"

"What do you mean, out of hand?"

"Keep away from them. They lose their good sense like the rest of us."

"What are they like?"

"They're beasts," he said calmly. Then he saw the calamari and linguini that the waiter had served. "Ah, *bene*," he gushed.

Rick began working on the escarole.

"The thing is," Mario said as he spooned the thin pasta around his fork, "you've got to start thinking Italian."

"How can I do that?"

"First of all, you've got to be suspicious of everybody. Don't trust anyone, especially people you're not related to. Next, always know where your wife is, at all times. A man is not a real man if he does not give his wife love and respect. Remember that."

"I adore Rosie."

"I know you do."

"But it's hard to keep track of her. She's a free woman."

"Nobody's free, Rick. That's something Italians know. And it's really important to know this."

"Mario, let's be candid."

"Okay," he agreed between mouthfuls of calamari. "Let's."

"My background never geared me up for this kind of life. I don't know whether I can handle it."

"What kind of life is that?" Mario asked, brimming with innocence.

"The way Italians live."

"What way?"

"All excitement."

Mario's eyes flashed with pride. "What did your background gear you up for?"

"A life of comfort and ease."

"Boring. Boring," Mario announced as he finished the calamari.

"We spent our summers in Maine. There, life is slow."

Mario grunted, not really listening, too intent on finishing the thin pasta.

"We spent most of the summer on our boat. My father loved his dream boat. That's all he thought about. We'd dock at the club and he'd get together with the owners of the other yachts. He'd talk about the design of boats and if he needed a new rudder and . . ." Rick paused, picking at a few zucchini, chomping on them, then swallowing them down. "His boat was the most important thing in the world, next to our land." Rick paused again. "I guess the land was always first."

"So?"

"The most exciting thing that happened to us was if our boat got caught in a squall and we had to limp into the harbor. That was our real tragedy. People would talk about it for months."

"And that's probably why your father came to SoHo," Mario observed.

"Mother said we came to SoHo because the major had a breakdown."

"I doubt it. He was probably bored. But what are you trying to tell me, kid? That you've made the wrong choice in life? I've known you since you were sixteen. Right?" Rick nodded. "You were always looking for action, only you didn't want anybody to know about it. You're still looking for action. When you run around SoHo in that dirty sweatsuit, what do you think you're doing?"

"Jogging."

"Crap," Mario said. "You're looking for action. Why don't you admit it?"

"That's simply not true."

"It is. You've got money, so you think, 'Okay, I can live a life doing nothing.' Right?" Mario didn't wait for Rick's answer. "Wrong."

"Mario, I was brought up to do nothing."

"What's the point of living, Ricky, baby, if you do nothing? It's okay for women, or it used to be. Children kept them busy. But not for men."

Rick flinched. Here was the real-man mystique again. Everybody seemed to know what a man was. The guys at the gym thought it meant getting it on with every available twat. His father, the major, thought a man was someone who could sail. Mario's version was that a man wanted action. This was probably Rosie's version, too.

"But *you* do nothing, now that you're retired."

"Not true. I'm clocking everything," Mario explained. "The only thing I'm retired from is going to the office. Everything else in my life, I still do. What do you think a man is? Simply a man who works? That's only part of it. That's the part to make the money to feed his family. But a man is more than that. He's the head of his family. But I forgot," he added snidely, "you don't want a family."

"It's not that we don't . . ."

"Then what is it? You and my daughter are going to write the book that is going to get you both killed and you're not even leaving me a grandchild."

"That's not what we want to do."

"What's *want* got to do with life. You've got obligations to the people in your life. Your family. Your community."

"But I must live according to my ideals."

"Those aren't yours, Ricky. Those are your crazy father's ideals. I remember the major. After he came to SoHo, he was nuts. It's lucky the Army took care of him."

"What are you saying, Mario?"

"I'm saying that you married my daughter because you didn't want to live the way your father taught you to live. I'm saying that you want more than that. You don't want to sit around on your ass and do nothing. You want to fight life. You want to be in the thick of it. Like we are," he said proudly.

"You think I can?"

"Of course. Why do you think we bother with you?"

Rick was touched by Mario's concern. "Thanks."

"All of us know you can make it. But you must look and listen first. Forget what your father taught you. He was all wrong. That went for Maine, but not for SoHo and the rest of the world, where people are hungry and homeless. You have to help out, Ricky. That's what it's all about."

"That's it."

"That's it in a nutshell."

Rick pondered this as Mario ordered a pot of espresso and a bottle of Sambucco, which was reserved only for him. Suddenly, the door opened and an unkempt Detective Arthur Kushel walked in. At the same moment, Fast Bob and his underage sweetheart decided to exit, still smooching. Kushel watched them, disgusted.

"Yes, sir?" the bartender asked.

Kushel pointed to Rick. Slowly, he walked to the table.

"I was looking for you," he said to Rick.

"Hello, Detective Kushel," Rick said politely. "Would you like to sit down?"

Rick pulled up a chair for Kushel, though he was aware of Mario's displeasure.

"I was looking for you because I have news." Kushel's fingers flicked nervously when he looked at Mario. "Hello, Mr. Caesare."

"Disturbing us at dinner," Mario said grimly. "I hope it's important."

"What's happened?" Rick asked.

"The hands have disappeared from the police lab," the detective announced angrily. His eyes narrowed as he watched Rick's reaction.

"You're kidding. How did that happen?"

"I don't know. I thought maybe you knew something."

Rick suddenly remembered the taped conversation Rosie had recorded. Then he realized that an Italian would never reveal this evidence to the police.

"Don't know anything."

"Why are you asking him these dumb questions?" Mario glared.

"You and your wife seem very interested in those hands," Kushel continued addressing Rick.

"Not enough to cause their disappearance," Rick said hastily.

Mario beamed at Rick's behavior.

"I'm not sure what your real interest in this case is, Mr. Ramsey. I've had you checked out. I must say, your background is impressive." Kushel looked at Mario. "Did you know that Mr. Ramsey's great-grandfather has a town named after him in Maine?"

"Really? Kid, is that true?"

"Sort of."

"Why didn't you ever tell us?"

"It's not important."

"It sure is," Kushel said. "The Ramseys have immaculate credentials. Major Ramsey was in the U. S. Army. The major's father was career Army too. They're an Army family. Good, responsible Americans."

"So?" Mario baited.

"I think it's most unfortunate that someone from that kind of family is mixed up with this kind of thing."

"What kind of thing?" Rick asked.

"You slime." Mario's voice boomed. "What you mean is that it's unfortunate that he's married to my daughter." His lips glistened. "What are you?" he hissed hatefully.

"Lithuanian," Kushel said nervously. "But what does that matter, Mr. Caesare?"

"Detective Kushel, could you tell me why you wanted to see me?" Rick asked, gearing up for a *mano a mano* with the Lithuanian.

"Thought you might like to know that there were a couple of street types hanging out when the guys who stole the hands came running out of the police lab."

"Don't you have guards at the lab?" Rick asked.

"Yeah. But bribery opens a lot of doors."

"I see."

"Well, see, these street guys . . . well, you know how it is in SoHo . . . the artists hang around the streets all the time. Anyway, we managed to get a couple of good sketches of the thieves. It seems one of them looks like you." Kushel pointed to Rick.

"Impossible," Mario grunted, toying with a piece of calamari that the waiter had not cleaned away. Rick saw that his father-in-law was deeply disturbed by Kushel's news.

"Where were you last night around two A.M.?" Kushel asked Rick.

"In bed."

"Alone?"

"I sleep with my wife."

"She'd lie for you."

"She doesn't have to. I was asleep."

"Did anybody see you, I mean, besides her?"

"For Christ's sake. We don't usually sleep in a group."

Kushel laughed obscenely. Under his breath, Mario swore. Rick felt nervous. Was this detective trying to prove that he took the hands when he had been trying his very best to get those damn hands out of his life? What was it about those hands? Were they his karma?

"We have a thorough search going on, Mr. Ramsey. We will find those hands," Kushel said.

Rick watched Mario pick up the leftover calamari and chew on it. Mario must have been agitated since he normally had impeccable table manners.

"I don't know where those hands are, Detective Kushel."

"Do you have any ideas?"

"I don't know. Why don't you try the coffins?" Rick said, joking.

Suddenly, Mario's face turned beet red, then stark purple. Rick poured a glass of water, but Mario began gagging. Kushel stood up quickly and put his short arms around Mario's massive chest, but they wouldn't fit.

"Help me," Kushel demanded.

Rick wound his long arms around his father-in-law's chest. Mario's eyes were bulging. He was choking.

"Pump," Kushel instructed Rick.

Seconds later, the calamari erupted from Mario's mouth. Quickly, he sat down. He took a handkerchief from his breastpocket to wipe the perspiration from his face. He unbuttoned his shirt, loosened his tie, slowly took off his jacket, and rolled up his shirt sleeves.

"Take it easy, Mr. Caesare," Kushel said. "Are you all right?"

"I'll be fine once you leave," Mario gasped. Then the waiter brought him a glass of seltzer water. Mario drank it slowly and said, "Thanks for the help. Now, either arrest us or leave us in peace."

Kushel smiled. "Yes, Mr. Caesare. I got what I came for."

"You did?" Mario was back to his old self.

"You'll be hearing from us," Kushel warned.

There was an awkward silence as Kushel walked to the doorway. Then he waved good-bye and disappeared out into the street.

Rick looked at Mario.

"Are you sure you're all right?"

"You know, kid. I keep talking to you, but I don't get anywhere."

"What's the matter now?"

"Are you stupid or something?"

"What?"

"Why did you do that?"

"Do what?"

"How did you know where the hands are?"

"What are you talking about?"

"How could you tell that cop?"

"Tell him what?"

"Where the hands are."

"Where are the hands?"

"What do you mean where are the hands?" Mario shouted.

14

"So what happened?" Rick asked.

"Darling, it's odd. I've been living in New York all my life and one movie meeting changed my view of this city."

Rosie was sitting up in bed, nude. Her flesh was blushy pink, exciting and desirable. Quickly, Rick stepped out of his briefs and tackled her.

"Wait a second." She giggled. "Let me tell you about the meeting."

"Later."

"No, now," she insisted.

Rick swore. Then he practiced the deep-breathing exercises his karate studies had taught him. These were disciplined tests, which he hoped would calm the continual excitement his wife created. A few seconds later, he was calm. Rosie touched his hand.

"Tell me about it," he said, knowing he would not be permitted to love his wife until she told him about the meeting, the writer in Rosie always dominating the woman.

"There I was on Madison Avenue because the meeting was at the Polo Lounge," she began. "Did you know that the Hotel Westbury has a Polo Lounge, like Beverly Hills does?"

"Nope."

Slowly she shook her head. "We live in seclusion in Soho. Anyhow, as I got out of the taxi, I spot Gloria Vanderbilt looking into Sonia Rykiel's boutique. She's wonderfully rich. When we get wonderfully rich, I'm going there, too."

"Okay."

"Anyhow, the next thing I know, Richard Gere is walking by in a Giorgio Armani outfit. I thought he lived in the Village. Well, then I see Ben Gazzara in a desert outfit. You know, the kind we used to wear." Rick nodded. "Then I pass Givenchy. Of course, I immediately think of Audrey Hepburn. Wasn't Givenchy her favorite designer? Or was it Balenciaga?"

"Mr. B."

"Rick, you're smart."

"My mother's only vice was fashion magazines."

She kissed his cheek.

"I couldn't believe the Madison Avenue shops. There was a shop showing jewelry as sculpture. That fabulous bookstore, Books & Company, had speakers playing Wagner. Everyone was very trendy and well dressed. I felt giddy. We really should go uptown once in a while."

"It's too crowded."

"We should go to Fifty-seventh Street. My favorite corner is where Tiffany's and Trump Tower are. I feel sexy just standing there."

Rick knew that when Rosie went to that corner, she became uncontrollably happy. More than once, they'd had to race down the street to the Steinway Piano Store because Rosie absolutely had to play a piano.

"Those Madison Avenue people are seriously rich," she continued. "Limousines line up, back to back. I looked into La Lingerie and fell in love with a swell nightie. But the cost . . ."

"How much?"

"Twelve hundred dollars."

"Did you buy it?"

She stared at Rick.

"Not yet, darling. After we make our fortune, I will."

"Your Madison Avenue outing cheered you up?"

She looked glum. "Not really. You know, all those people are coming to SoHo now. You can't find walking space on West Broadway any longer. And the boutiques are charging as much as La Lingerie. We're definitely a status area."

"It's awful."

"It kills me when I think about the souls of the Italian immigrants who used to sweat in SoHo factories. My grandmother used to clean floors in the dead of night. Poor woman. She had nine children and had to clean office floors so her family could eat."

Rick held Rosie close. "Tell me about the meeting," he said.

"Huh?" She was lost in memories.

"The meeting with the Hollywood people?"

"Oh."

At will, Rosie moved back through a veil that separated time. Her past memories were so vivid that she would physically relive them. Rick suspected that Rosie actually left her body when immersed by SoHo ghosts. He knew the past could often take Rosie from him. It happened whenever she sat at the typewriter. There, she existed outside the present, where voices from her past called. Rick worried. Suppose there was a fire when she was writing? Would she hear the siren? Probably not. That's why Rick hung around, to protect his love. But he was at a loss when memories held on. Rosie looked different at those times. Later, she would remember everything in great detail. Her grandparents' early struggles. Her SoHo childhood. Sometimes these memories seemed to be stronger than her present life. Whenever this happened, Rick was gentle with her.

"The meeting?" he hinted.

She laughed, back to reality. "Those movie types are odd," she observed. "I've always loved the movies. Even when we were poor, Dad took me to the Loew's Sheridan on

Greenwich Avenue. If I hadn't become a writer, I would have become a movie star."

"You could have. You're beautiful," he whispered.

"You could, too. You're better-looking than 'Magnum.'"

"Nobody's better-looking than Tom."

"You are, darling," she whispered.

"The movie people?"

"Right. Well, movies have always been my number-one hobby. Yours, too, right, Rick?" He nodded. "Well, I've got bad news. The people who make movies are strange."

"How strange?"

"They don't communicate. Do you know, nobody talked about the book." She gushed happily. "But it's great to have movie interest."

"Want to celebrate?"

Rick put his tongue in Rosie's mouth.

"Wait a sec. Let me tell you about the movie meeting first."

"Okay. Okay."

Rick practiced the Eastern meditation, which actually did calm things even though his erection remained quite active.

"We spent the first half hour talking about the best exercise person in Beverly Hills. Do you know that Lana Murphy, a free-lance muscle creator, can push a woman's weight down to a hundred and ten pounds in only three weeks?"

"Huh?"

"Mrs. Mazel told me that. She's the wife half of the Arthur Mazel Inc. team that wants to buy the rights to the hands book—"

"The hands book?" Rick interrupted Rosie.

"That's what they're calling it."

"Ughhhh."

"I know. I tried to explain that the book is much more than the hands, but Miles stopped me. He said it's okay, those movie people have to have a handle on a project. Apparently, they have so much on their minds that they get confused easily. So I shut up. Our book is called the hands book."

"Hands! Hands! Hands!" Rick jumped up and down on the mattress, shouting, "Those hands are making me crazy."

"Your erection is going," Rosie observed.

"Those hands will do that."

"Come back down, darling."

He did as she asked. He'd gotten into the habit of jumping up and down on the bed when he was young. He didn't remember how or when it began. But he had many confused memories about his childhood. Terrible things must have happened, he often thought, because he couldn't remember much.

He sat next to Rosie and his erection blew up again. Rick sighed happily. It was good to know that his equipment was working.

She continued. "Anyhow, Mrs. Mazel said she gets most of her exercise swimming in her pool and dancing at deal parties."

"Deal parties?"

"She says she makes the best deals dancing the Cuban rumba."

"That's a Forties dance."

"She says it's back in. That and the lindy. Mrs. M. says everything starts in California, and New York should be following suit at the end of the year."

"Did she say anything else?"

"She said jogging was bad for women and that she hates all athletes except for Tom Selleck."

"I told you everybody loves Tom."

"She says he has great legs."

"He does."

"So do you, baby. They'd love you, too, but I'm not going to share you with anyone. Will you remember that?"

Rick kissed her, pleased with her obsessive passion, which he could not live without.

"Then she began about the Queen," Rosie said.

"What queen?"

"It seems that the Queen went to Los Angeles and that

made everybody gloomy. Fast Bob Talbot gave a party for those who were not invited to the Queen's luncheon. Guess what? Nobody came."

"But his parties are famous?"

"Everybody said they were out of town."

"Why?"

"Apparently, the rents on Rodeo Drive are changing the life in Beverly Hills."

He was confused. "The rents on Rodeo Drive?"

"That's what Mrs. M. spent the next half hour telling me. She says that the Trigere Boutique has moved from the Drive. She says that the punkers with Mohawk haircuts go to a new spot called the City Cafe."

"There's one on Prince Street."

"Right. This must be the West Coast branch. Mrs. M. says she never lunches there. She lunches at Ma Maison because the Paramount people go there. The CBS crowd goes to the Cadillac Cafe because they like pasta."

"What about the book?" Rick was exasperated.

"Wait a sec. Mrs. M. talked about how downtown L.A. was changing. All the artists have lofts there, like in SoHo. And Perino's is opening a large complex. And there's a new place, called Gorky's Cafe, which will serve Russian caviar, like the Russian Tea Room does." Rosie sighed. "I love the Russian Tea Room because it's on Fifty-seventh Street."

"Okay."

"Then Mrs. M. started on caviar. While she was talking about caviar, Mr. M. arrived."

"What's he like?"

"He's slim and wears horn-rimmed glasses and is probably fifty but looks thirty-five."

"Mrs. M?"

"She looks like a former chorus girl who has had a sex lift."

"A sex lift?"

"That's when someone doesn't know whether they want

to be a man or a woman and they pick something in-between."

"Rosie, stop that."

"Sorry. That's how it seemed to me. I couldn't tell what she was, even with her long red hair sprinkled with sequins."

"At lunch?"

"Madison Avenue is awfully boffy these days," she conceded.

Rick wondered whether the modern world had finally gone mad. The Ramseys would never allow sequins at lunch. In fact, they'd never allow sequins ever, except, perhaps, on New Year's Eve and only if a family member was traveling on an ocean liner in mid-sea.

"So you got to talking about the deal?" Rick urged.

"That's not what happened."

Rosie's nipples seemed appetizing, so Rick licked one. Suddenly it pointed straight ahead.

"Rick, don't do things like that when we're talking business."

"Let's get to business then," he suggested.

"But we didn't. Mr. M. joined us as Mrs. M. was telling us about caviar. Did you know that caviar is the world's most expensive food?"

"Yes."

"Did you know that awful people are beginning to put dye in caviar so the Hollywood crowd has to hire taste experts to tell whether it's real or not?"

"You're joking."

"No, I'm not. Caviar tasting has become the newest cottage industry in L.A."

"How do they train?"

"That's a good question. Mr. M. says his tasters know exactly when the sturgeon is caught, how the eggs are processed, how much salt is used. Quite impressive, isn't it?"

"Rosie. Did anyone ever talk about the book?"

"Then Mr. M. ordered a kirsch and cassis de Paris."

"A what?"

"It's a drink with—"

"Never mind."

"And Mrs. M. ordered a raspberry quencher, which she said she was introduced to at the Four Seasons."

"And Miles?"

"Miles drank straight vodka. You know how he is."

"Authentic."

"Right."

"The deal?"

"When the meeting was over, Miles and I went to a coffee shop to talk."

"What did he say?"

"He said that the meeting had gone awfully well."

"What?"

"Yes. Apparently when I went to the ladies room, Mr. and Mrs. Mazel agreed to option the book, even though it isn't written yet. They're going for twenty thou, with a guaranteed upward scale if it hits the best-seller list."

"How much then?"

"It goes quite high."

"How high?"

"Half a mil."

"Great."

"And if they finally make the film, then we could make serious money."

"Whew."

"But, Rick, I didn't accept the deal."

"What?" he screamed. "I thought that's what you wanted."

"I told Miles that we absolutely had to write the screenplay."

"My God, you didn't."

"Why not? We've been going to the movies all our lives. I'm sure we could write a wonderful film."

"We haven't written the book yet."

"What's that got to do with it?"

"Oh, right."

"Don't worry, Rick. Miles said he'd demand that as part of the deal."

"Will Mr. and Mrs. M. agree?"

"If they don't, we're back to square one."

"Honey, does it matter that much to you?"

"Everything matters that much."

"Enough to give up the deal?"

"Uh-huh."

What courage, Rick thought, as he pressed his dry hot lips upon Rosie's sweet moist ones. His lady was not only sexy and beautiful, she also had ideals and a sense of honor. Every cell in his body came alive as he sank into the mist of loving her.

The next few days were unusually calm. This was a rarity, for since Rick had known Rosie, life was always filled with surprises, traumas, and dramatic events. In the years he'd lived with her, in both sin and marriage, he'd come to expect, and yes, even demand, a daily Italian drama. Whenever their life changed into a dull pattern of waking up and going through the day without a major catastrophy, Rick worried. Always his worry transformed itself into intense erotic cravings, and he plotted to take Rosie whenever and however he could. And he did. Passionately, they loved on the new black-tile bathroom floor, with Rosie's head hitting the thick red plush carpet edge as he repeatedly showed his love for her. They loved in the elevator, as Rick prayed that Arnoldo would not turn his energy transport on and discover them. They even loved in Washington Square Park underneath the statue of Garibaldi, where they wore loose Indian garments and pretended they were struggling against the early summer wind. But they weren't. They were getting it on.

The excesses of Rick's nervousness lasted all week.

"Wow," Rosie said, one morning. "You're really hot. You must be churning on about something."

"You're always hot."

"I'm always churned on to life."

"Let's go to the park and get it on in front of the NYU library."

"We'll get arrested."

"Can they arrest us if we're married?"

"Think so."

"They changed the law. I think it's okay for married people."

"Then I'm not going to do it anymore. It's more fun when it's wrong."

They laughed.

"But we've got to stop or we're not going to get our work done," she scolded.

"You're not," Rick corrected.

"Nope, you too. I've got a schedule mapped out. Today I've got to interview one of the guards at the police lab. A friend of Aunt Irene's claims he might know something about the missing hands."

"What?"

"They never talk on the phone. Funny thing is, they don't mind talking into tape recorders."

"It's because of those gangster movies. They didn't have tape recorders in the Thirties."

"Maybe. What are you planning to work on?"

"Nothing."

"Wrong. You've got to cover the cemetery."

"Not me."

"The *Post* says the cops are digging up the coffins today."

"They won't let me in the cemetery."

"Find a way."

Rick pondered how to accomplish his assignment. How could he get into the cemetery? He could pretend that he was a jogger who had discovered that the presence of dead souls calmed his jagged nerves. No. That wouldn't do. Kushel would recognize him in his sweatsuit. He could dress up as a cop. No. Too risky. And illegal. Maybe he could be a maintenance man. Nobody noticed them. Rick liked that idea. He went to his closet. During the Seventies, he used to dress like someone on Army maintenance duty. Yes, his old clothes were perfect. He got into fatigues. He looked okay. All he needed was a shovel to be completely in character.

He left the loft and jogged down to Canal Street, where he bought a used shovel. Then he took the subway. Ordinarily, Rick never took the subway, but it would be in character for a maintenance worker to do this. He had to find St. Joseph's Cemetery in Queens. Rick had never been to Queens, but the token-booth person said it was relatively simple to find. It was only five stations away. Where had Rick gotten the idea that Queens was far away? The station was marked clearly: St. Joseph's Place. He got off. There was a sign that read ST. JOSEPH'S CEMETERY. It was a short walk from the station. Queens was like California. Everyone was in a car or waiting for a bus. Nobody walked. Rick walked fast, hoping the shovel was a good cover. No one seemed to notice him. At the entrance to the cemetery, a group of press people waited for news. Rick mingled. Inside, the police had roped off the section where the Salernos were buried. Casually, Rick strolled past two cops who were smoking a reefer.

"Something special happening?" Rick asked.

"We're digging up a couple of stiffs," one cop said.

"Dago stiffs," the other laughed.

"Can I cut through this way?"

"Where're you off to?"

"Got to dig a grave." Rick motioned to the shovel.

"Okay. Go that way," the cop said as he took another toke. Rick crossed under the rope.

"Why are you digging them up?" Rick asked from the other side of the rope.

"We're looking for something."

Rick swore under his breath, hoping they wouldn't find what they were looking for. St. Joseph's was an old cemetery. The gravestones were huge. These days, nobody could afford them. Many had large angels and saints sculpted on top.

Some had intricate marble fences around them. Rick checked a few dates. Most of the gravestones had been put there at the beginning of this century. He found a large one that had a huge statue of an archangel to protect the deceased, a Mr. Samuel Sloan. Rick hid behind the angel's feet. From there, he could see the maintenance workers digging up the ground. It was hard work in the sun. He waited patiently. An hour later, they were still digging. Rick was getting tired. He knew that he would not have made a good stakeout detective. Maybe Mario was right. Maybe he needed action. Maybe he thrived on it, even while he complained. Or maybe knowing Rosie had changed him.

Suddenly, something happened. The diggers stopped and cops milled about excitedly. Rick hid, secure behind the archangel's large feet, where he could see everything clearly. Kushel appeared, surrounded by beefy men in suits. Other detectives, Rick decided. Kushel ordered one to open the coffins. "Oh, no," Rick swore, glad that he could not actually see the coffins. Kushel pointed to one coffin. One of his beefy pals bent down and picked something out of it. Then he put it into a large plastic bag. He walked over to the other coffin and did the same thing. Rick turned and vomited right on poor Mr. Sloan's grave. He knew what the beefy detective had put into the bags.

Damn those hands. They were back in circulation.

15

The slim woman in the dark hat followed Rosie discreetly. Bond Street was a three-block oasis, off Broadway. There was little traffic in this enclave, and huge tractor trailer trucks used it as a private parking lot. Carefully, the woman observed Rosie's white suit lighting up Bond Street's soot and grime.

A man in a doorway called out to Rosie. Quickly, she followed him and disappeared.

The slim woman wondered who the man was. She would have to find out, because he was probably telling the reporter something about the rooftop murders. The gossip in SoHo was that Rosie was going to write a book on this incident. Fat chance. She'd never live to see its publication.

Patiently, the woman waited. Two drunks rambled by, turned, spotted her, and begged for coins. But they sped on. Something about her frightened them. A truck drove noisily down the street. Two cats chased each other from a window ledge to the roof of a building.

She decided that this place was perfect.

The woman opened her alligator bag and took out a strong cord. She wound her fingers about one end, then the other. She pulled the cord taut. Yes, this would do very nicely for Rosie's neck.

She felt the eager anticipation of pleasure strike something very deep within her. A flush traveled throughout her strong body. The reporter would beg for mercy. How her eyes would bulge. How her pretty face would pale. How her skin tone would discolor as the cord was tightened around her neck. Terror would make her ugly.

Her lover would never look at Rosie's face again.

A few moments later, Rosie came out of the doorway. Carefully looking up the street, she decided to return the same way she'd come.

Good, the woman thought. It was easy. She hid among the shadows as Rosie's heels tapped down the concrete street. As the reporter swept by, the slim woman surged forward. Quickly, she wound the cord around Rosie's throat. Rosie struggled, but her attacker's hold was invincible. The woman drew the cord tighter as Rosie gasped for life.

Then a man's voice called out that Rosie had forgotten her tape recorder. Quickly, the slim woman spun the cord from Rosie's throat. Like a panther, she fled down the street and disappeared.

16

"Rosie," Rick asked, "are you okay?"

She'd arrived home shaky and disheveled, explaining that she'd taken a bad fall.

"Damn heels," she cursed.

But her teeth were chattering. He put his arms around her and held her.

"Take it easy."

She was trembling as he guided her to the sofa. There, he took her hands into his, rubbing them softly against his lips.

"What can I do?"

"Damn," she hissed.

"Hey, you're really boiling."

"I'll be okay."

She sat on the sofa. Her eyes were half-closed and he could see she was furious. Then she jumped up and began pacing.

"We've got to get action on this caper. We'll shock those beasts and flush them out. I'm going to call Stacey."

Stacey Wilson lived in SoHo with a ballerina, an opera singer, and a stewardess. The opera singer was working on a secret novel and was in love with the stewardess. The ballerina was Stacey's lover, though it was rumored in SoHo that the group was living in a menage. Stacey never confirmed this and tried to keep her personal life private; as a leading anchorperson on UBC Cable News, she had to.

"Remember, honey. Mario said to be careful who we talk to."

"Don't be a coward."

"I'm being realistic."

Rick took the phone from her. Rosie was so angry that she socked him.

"Hey, stop that," he protested.

She jumped up from the couch. "You're a coward," she shouted. "You've always been a coward. Remember when you began making it with Sharon? Did you come home to me and say, 'Well, Rosie, I've fallen for another woman'? No. You simply disappeared. The next thing I knew a friend called and said that you'd married that tramp. Coward!" she shouted, still furious. "They grow cowards in New England."

"Rosie, stop this."

"You never even phoned me. I thought you might be dead. I was sitting there, wondering who to call when I got the news." She sucked in her fury, then hurled it out at him again. "You left all your clothes. I had to live for eight years with your sweaters and socks. I thought when we married, it would make a difference. But it hasn't. You're still a coward."

"Shit. Stop saying that."

"Then stop acting like one." Her eyes filled with angry, bitter tears. "For God's sake. This is hard enough for me. I need you."

He took her into his arms and tried to calm her down.

"What do you want me to do?" he finally asked.

"Come with me to UBC. We'll give Stacey the tape to air."

"If we do that, the police will arrest us."

"We'll stand behind the First Amendment. We're journalists."

"If I do it, will you admit that I'm not a coward?"

"Absolutely." She smiled.

"Let's go then."

With his decision, she cheered up quickly. "Let's both wear beige," she quipped.

"Why beige?"

"Because people think they can see through beige," she explained, rummaging through the closet.

A half hour later, they were both dressed in their *Casablanca* motif, beige raw linen suits and panama straw hats. Everything matched.

Downstairs, Rick hailed a cab and they soon arrived at the UBC building. When they walked into the lobby, a security guard stopped them.

"Have to search your bag," he said. "Just had a bomb threat."

Rosie had hidden the tape in her bra, which made her seem bustier than usual. She handed the guard her large bag. After the search, he asked, "Who are you going to see?"

"Stacey Wilson. Tell her the Ramseys want to see her."

He called Stacey's office and confirmed the fact that the Ramseys could visit.

"Twenty-ninth floor," he said, giving them both a large pass to wear on their lapels.

On the twenty-ninth floor, the receptionist told them where Stacey's office was located. They found Stacey sitting behind a desk littered with wire tear sheets, reference books, and cartons of Chinese food. A cigarette jutted from her lips. Her sneakers, old corduroy trousers, and owl glasses proved that she refused to be glamorous. Some media people thought Stacey was a madwoman.

"Is this a social visit?" Stacey asked when they entered. "You know I don't believe in socializing with my SoHo friends. They all have sexually transmittable diseases," she joked.

"You're warped, Stacey," Rosie said.

"Yeah, but I make tons of money." She laughed and picked up a large bucket of popcorn. "Have some corn. I'm gaining pounds and pounds. I've been editing a documentary and can't break my childhood habit of eating popcorn when I watch film. Silly, isn't it?"

"Stacey. We're here on professional business," Rosie announced.

Stacey's eyes opened wide. "What kind of professional business?" she asked.

"We're covering the rooftop murders for a book," Rick began.

"Yes. I know. News travels fast. Congratulations. I understand you have a film deal."

"Uh-huh," Rick said.

"We've got something terrific for you," Rosie added.

"What?"

"A tape with important stuff," Rosie continued.

"What kind of important stuff?"

"A certain person announced on tape that he's going to steal those dead hands back from the cops," Rosie explained.

"What certain person?"

"Can't say," Rosie declared.

"Come on, Rosie," Stacey complained. She looked at Rick. "Rick?" she asked.

He shrugged his shoulders.

"If you're not going to tell me who the person is, how do I know it's authentic?" Stacey asked.

"Play it," Rick said quietly.

Stacey took the tape from Rosie. Her bookcase was lined with electronic equipment of all types. Quickly, she put the cassette into a tape player and pressed a button. She wrinkled her nose at the tape's fuzziness, but when she heard the last voice, she grew excited.

"That sounds like Borgotta," she observed.

Rick and Rosie remained silent.

"Is it Vito Borgotta?" Stacey asked.

"That's up to UBC," Rosie answered.

"I'll have my boss listen to this. May I keep it?"

"Can you make a copy while we wait? We want to keep the original," Rosie said.

"Wait a minute," Stacey said. "If this is an exclusive tape, why are you giving it to UBC?"

"We have our reasons," Rick answered.

When they were alone, he turned to Rosie. "Darling, what are our reasons?"

"Italians love headlines, Rick. When this tape is aired, the media is going to swarm into SoHo and somebody is going to talk."

"Wait a sec. I thought you said they won't talk."

"They won't talk when they think they have to be loyal. But when the cops know the facts, the Italians don't mind talking a little bit as long as they don't divulge anything new."

"How is this going to help us?"

"Someone will crack," she observed.

"I don't know whether I agree."

"Believe me, darling. I know my people."

"We should call Mario."

"I'll try." She dialed quickly. "Dad. Where've you been? You were in Southampton, visiting Aunt Irene. How is she? Look, Dad, I'm at UBC. I'm talking to a reporter friend of mine about the murders. What? Who told you about the tape?"

Exasperated, she handed the phone to Rick. "He wants to talk to you."

At the other end of the phone, Mario was furious. "Kid, stop her. I've gotten the word that you're in trouble. Do you understand?"

"Rosie thinks I'm a coward."

"Then be one. Stop her, or you won't have a wife much longer, kid."

Suddenly, overwhelming anxiety gripped Rick's heart. He couldn't live without Rosie.

"Did you hear me, kid?" Mario repeated.

Rick began shaking. Nothing could take his Rosie from him. His entire body felt like whipped cream and, to his surprise, his equipment became fully erect. He pressed against his love.

"Not here," Rosie said, feeling him hard against her.

Rick turned away, puzzled that extreme fear would cause an erection.

"Remember," Mario continued, "nobody believes you didn't really know the dead hands were in the coffin when you ratted to that Lithuanian."

"What do you want me to do?"

"Stop her."

"I'll try."

"Don't try. Do it, kid."

"Okay."

"Remember, Ricky, it's all up to you now."

Rick hung up the phone feeling sick.

"I've got to take a leak, Rosie. Be right back," he said, forming a quick plan. He ran down the hall until he found the tape library. Inside, Stacey was working on the tape.

"Stacey. There's a phone call for you. It's urgent," he lied.

"Rick, watch this, will you?"

"Sure, honey."

"Be right back."

As soon as she was gone, Rick pressed down the stop button on the recorder and the copier. Then he took out both cassettes and put them inside his pocket. Swiftly, he left the library. He found the men's room a few doors down the hall. He entered. No one was about. Quickly, he put both tapes into the sink and torched them. As he watched the black cinders, he felt rotten. Rosie was right. He was a coward. But he had to save her. Nothing was worth losing his darling. Suddenly he started to laugh hysterically. After all these years of knowing Rosie, he was finally thinking Italian.

17

"I'll kill you, you son of a bitch!"

Rick ran down the hallway, followed by Rosie waving two clenched fists. Fortunately, the UBC elevator car arrived. He hopped onto it. There were three people in the car, two men and a petite woman wearing a strange hat with two tall feathers. Accidentally, Rick stepped on the woman's foot.

"Sorry," he apologized.

"A pleasure," she responded, her brown cowlike eyes slipping into a sensuous mood.

Rick pressed the lobby button and prayed that the doors would shut before Rosie caught up, but his luck was bad. As the doors closed, Rosie's shapely foot appeared. Immediately, the doors opened for her.

"Son of a bitch," she shouted. "I'll kill you. You coward. You beast." Rosie slammed Rick's head with her large raw silk *Casablanca* bag, breaking Rick's Panama straw hat in two.

"See what you've done," he said, immediately depressed, holding the torn hat close to his heart.

They'd bought the twin Panama straw hats at a New Paltz flea market. An elderly couple had kept the hats in their attic while waiting for their sons to return from World War II. When the couple decided that their sons were never returning home, they sold the hats. Rick and Rosie bought them, vowing a solemn pact to wear the hats only when they were madly happy.

Sadly, Rick looked down at the broken Panama hat. Subdued now, Rosie took his arm.

"Ricky. I'm sorry about the hat."

"It's gone forever. Our *Casablanca* fantasy is washed up."

"We'll buy another one."

"It won't be the same."

Rick put the hat up to his tear-stained cheek and kissed its rim. The two male passengers, dressed in gray Brooks Brothers cotton, laughed.

"What's wrong?" Rosie asked hostily. "Never seen a man cry?" She put her arms protectively around Rick. "Well, real men cry."

The lady in the feather hat gushed. "What an ass," she said pointedly.

"You're asking for it. All of you shut up," Rosie declared.

Her command of the car's passengers was instantaneous. Obviously, the men did not want anything to spoil their lunch. The woman seemed genuinely afraid. Under her feathers, she whispered a mantra. When the car arrived at the lobby, the woman ran out at once and grabbed a security guard.

"Come on, speed up," Rosie said to Rick, crashing through the revolving doors. Outside, she hailed a cab. "Downtown," she said to the driver once they were safely inside.

"Lady, where do you want to go?"

"I told you."

"Downtown is a big place. Where downtown?"

The lady with the feathers and the security guard were coming through UBC's doors in hot pursuit.

"Get a move on, buddy." Rosie sounded warped as she issued sinister threats.

"Tell me where . . ."

"Follow that car." She pointed to a gray Mercedes-Benz pulling away from the curb.

Obediently, the driver raced after the car. They headed uptown.

"You fool. You fool," Rosie whispered to Rick.

"I want my hat," he moaned.

"Hey, that car is turning onto the bridge," the driver observed.

"Go downtown," Rosie ordered.

Abruptly, the cab stopped in front of Bloomingdale's. The traffic was horrendous. There were several sleek limos double-parked, causing utter confusion because the city buses could not stop at bus stops.

"Damn," the driver swore.

"Broadway and Houston. That's where we want to go," Rosie offered.

"Thank you, lady," the driver said impatiently. Then he hurled the cab into the crosstown traffic, which brought them to a full stop.

"What's wrong?" Rosie asked.

"Can't you see what's wrong? Women!" the driver complained, throwing his hands up into the air.

"Lorenzo, don't be a pig." Rosie had read the driver's name on the identifying plate.

"Mr. Gomez to you, lady," he replied, lighting up a big black cigar. When fumes reached the back seat, Rosie began coughing.

"Don't do that," she complained.

"Lady, this is my cab."

Rick hid under his broken Panama hat, moaning for his *Casablanca* dream.

"What's the matter with him?" the driver asked.

"Nothing."

"Did you beat him up?"

"I should have," Rosie said, reflecting her continued fury.

"Women are cowards," the driver announced. The traffic began moving with much horn-blowing and cursing, Manhattan style. "The thing is," the driver said, puffing on his cigar as he waved through the traffic using only one finger on the wheel, "when men used to beat women, women put up a fuss."

"What do you mean, used to? They still do," Rosie replied.

"Maybe. But those men are beasts."

"Oh"—Rosie was interested now—"why did you use that word?"

"Huh?"

Swearing at the driver of a Macy's truck, which seemed to want to crush his cab, the cabdriver swerved onto the sidewalk and sped down it, causing shocked pedestrians to run out of his path. When the cab reached Park Avenue, it turned abruptly. Immediately, the pace changed. Park Avenue boasted a better type of cab driver—those who shouted "Damn" instead of the unmentionable curses heard on Third Avenue. But the horns, the traffic, the driver's black cigar smoke, and Rosie's anger were getting to Rick anyway.

"Life is hell," he moaned. Savagely, he crushed the Panama hat into small pieces.

"What are you doing?" Rosie screamed. "We could have had it mended."

"No way."

She took off her Panama hat and handed it to Rick.

"Take mine."

"It won't fit."

"It falls down over my ears. Try it."

Rick tried the hat on. It felt too small, but Rosie insisted that he check it out in her compact mirror.

"Looks like Bogie," he observed. "I'm more the Mitchum type."

"We both know you're Tom."

"I'm Selleck in a baseball cap, but I'm Mitchum in a Panama."

"Okay, you're Mitchum. Driver, stop the cab."

"Why here?" Rick asked.

"We could walk over to Third Avenue and look for another hat. I'll give it to you for your birthday."

"My birthday isn't for months."

"For Christmas then."

"It's summer."

"Then for no reason except that I love you."

"Do you?"

"Yes."

"Then you've forgiven me for the tape?"

Instantly, Rick realized he'd made a mistake. When Rosie remembered why the hat had been destroyed in the first place, she rolled up her right fist into a ball and socked Rick. Blood gushed from his nose.

"Lady, you're nuts! Get out of my cab," the driver shouted.

"Take us to Houston and Broadway," Rosie ordered.

"Hey, guy? You want me to call a cop?"

"No," Rick said, thick with blood. "Got a handkerchief?"

"Take this box of Kleenex."

Rick sopped up his blood with Kleenex.

"Aren't you going to sock her back?" the driver asked.

"Go ahead," Rosie declared, with both fists ready. "I knew you'd hit me someday."

"No way. I'll never hit you. I want you to remember that always."

"Aw, Ricky." She softened. "What am I going to do with you?"

"She's really nuts," the driver observed. "I'd never take that from a dame."

"Drive on," Rick insisted. "This is between us."

"It's your dough." The driver nervously put one finger back on the wheel.

"Rick?"

"I'm not talking to you," he answered, continuing to sop up his blood.

"Here, take this," she said softly, handing him a handkerchief.

"Don't bother."

He was really mad at her. Fun was fun, but nosebleeds were serious stuff. He'd had them throughout his childhood. Everytime he even thought of a nosebleed, fear gripped his body. Now he felt total panic, and noted, with clinical detail, that panic did not produce an erection.

"Darling."

But Rick was not moved. Enough was enough. Being married to a feminist was difficult, but being married to an Italian was sometimes impossible.

The driver pulled up in front of their building.

"Damn," Rosie swore as she paid the fare. "There's Dad."

Mario was pacing back and forth with a worried expression on his face. He was dressed in Southampton fashion: white slacks and white open shirt, with a gold chain around his neck. Next to him, leaning stoically against the Pappas Occult Bookstore, was Aunt Irene.

"Where the hell you been?" Mario rushed over to the cab. When he opened the door, Rick fell into his arms. "Did they get you? Where are you shot? Get this guy to a hospital," he ordered the confused cabdriver.

The driver nonchalantly waved Mario away. "The dame did it," he explained.

Aunt Irene waddled over. "Ricky, baby, what has my niece done to you?"

"I socked him," Rosie announced.

People began staring. Even in SoHo, blood made an impression.

"Let's get inside," Mario said, observing the crowd.

A few minutes later, they huddled in the elevator car while Irene sopped up Rick's blood with her delicate Irish lace handkerchief.

"There, there, Ricky," she cooed. "Rosie, you always had a bad temper."

"She never had a bad temper. She was always a lady," Mario insisted.

"She's like you, Mario. Hotheaded and too quick to act. If you hadn't been hotheaded, we wouldn't be in this mess."

"My brother was hotheaded too," Mario said. "And you loved him."

"I adored Iggie," she agreed.

"His name was Ignatius," Mario corrected.

"Rick, you're still bleeding," Irene observed.

"No, it's stopped," Rick said hopefully. She took the handkerchief from his nose, but the blood continued. "Oh, God, I'm going to die," Rick said, feeling faint.

Suddenly, the car started to go haywire. "Arnoldo!" Rosie cried. "Ricky, what's your crazy friend doing now?"

"Don't know. Don't care," Rick answered. He was being drained of his life force, right here in his very own elevator car, and Arnoldo wouldn't even let them land.

"Oh, God," Irene said. "I'm going to throw that crazy Arnoldo out on his ass."

Suddenly, the elevator car stopped. When the door opened, their neighbor Max stepped in. As usual, he was dressed in soiled overalls. Today they were spotted with fresh sky-blue paint.

"Hello," Max said to all.

"Jesus Christ, you idiot. Look what you've done," Irene screeched as the elevator car began to rise. "You slob . . . you swine . . ." she continued.

The pink cashmere sweater Irene was holding was covered with paint from Max's sky-blue paint brush, which he'd accidentally hit her with. In retribution, Irene raised her chunky fist and hit Max square in the nose. Carefully, Rick watched, noting that Max did not bleed. Instead, his nose turned blush red. Max was furious, but he spotted Mario staring at him.

"We don't hit ladies when I'm around," Mario announced.

Mario's edict was accepted because he was physically

stronger than poor Max. Irene moaned. Rick watched her through his bloody maze. As usual, Irene was dressed like a cross between a Park Avenue hooker and a 1946 movie musical star gone to fat. Her shocking-pink silk dress bellowed from the waist down. Above the waist, its halter style revealed Irene's plump shoulders. Around her neck, she wore a genuine pearl choker, rumored to be her present husband's legacy from his great-grandmother. The old dowager had given these pearls to Charlie Campton, who gave them to every woman he married. Of course, Charlie always reclaimed them after the divorce, but Irene liked the rare pearls around her throat and vowed that Charlie would never get them back.

Irene's shoes had very high heels of the Joan Crawford platform type, her usual style. Her plump, dimpled legs were covered with pink patterned stockings, the kind Rick had seen only on Parisian courtesans in Impressionist paintings. On her fingers she wore two rings. Both were huge diamonds, which glinted now against the pink cashmere sweater she held. Rick wondered why Irene would dress in her usual 1946 cocktail party motif on such a hot and humid day.

"At last," she moaned when the car stopped at their floor. Gingerly, she stepped past Max. Rosie helped Rick, while Mario acted as rear guard. When they left the car, Max began swearing in Swedish.

"Watch your mouth," Mario cautioned as he locked the door behind him.

"Impossible sap," Irene commented. "Rosie, where's your Woolite?"

"Are you going to wash your sweater out now?" Rosie asked.

"I can get this blue paint off if I soak it immediately."

"Buy a new one, Aunt Irene. You can afford it. Call Bergdorf's. Ask them to messenger down a dozen."

"Watch your mouth," her aunt cautioned as she rummaged through the kitchen until she found the Woolite. Then, humming "The Man I Love," she soaked the sweater.

"Let's get Ricky cleaned up," Mario suggested.

Rosie disappeared. When she returned, she held a damp washcloth and a shirt. Gingerly, she cleaned up Rick's face and handed him the new shirt. Then she handed the blood-stained shirt to Irene. "Put this in the Woolite."

"Do your own soaking," her aunt retorted, carefully washing the pink cashmere. "Do you have a large towel? I need a large towel," she demanded.

"Screw you," Rosie answered. "Rick, can I get you anything?"

"A new wife," her aunt countered.

Mario poured a Coke into an elegant cocktail glass. "Here, kid, have a Coke."

"Give it to Rosie. She needs it."

Rick watched Rosie gulp the Coke down. She was really an addict. He knew that the Coca Cola Company owned Columbia Pictures. Maybe Coke would buy the rights to their book because of Rosie's addiction.

"Let's all sit down," Mario commanded.

Irene rolled the precious cashmere sweater into a large bath towel and put it on the piano to dry.

"The piano will warp," Rosie said, picking up the towel.

"You leave my sweater alone." Irene waddled over to Rosie, but her niece was too swift. She grabbed the towel and disappeared.

"It's okay," Rosie said when she returned. "I've laid it on Ishtar."

"What's Ishtar?" her aunt asked.

"She's an Indian goddess."

"Would you women stop this nonsense," Mario ordered impatiently. "We have important things to talk about."

"Did she really sock you?" Irene asked Rick.

"Rosie, did you sock the kid?" Mario asked Rosie.

"He torched my tapes."

"Good for him," Mario observed.

"It was evidence," she insisted.

"Dangerous evidence. I told Rick that you're both in

trouble." He turned to Rick. "Kid, I don't want my daughter to be alone from now on. Understand?" Rick nodded.

Rosie's eyelashes flickered as she looked at Rick with her incredibly beautiful green eyes. "Is that why you did it?" she asked him.

"Something like that," he answered.

"I didn't know. But you were wrong."

"Don't sock me again." Rick put his arms up to his face. "It's not fair. You know I can't hit back."

"Why not?" Irene asked.

"Because he's a man," Mario pronounced.

Rick's shoulders swelled up and his head reeled. Suddenly the bleeding and headache disappeared. Had he heard right? Had Mario pronounced his manhood finally? He jumped up from the couch and ran the entire length of the loft. Then he picked up a stray slipper and pretended that it was a football. He tossed it to Mario, who caught it and tossed it back. Then Rick swerved and gracefully accomplished a beautiful touchdown. He was on the football field. He was a hero again.

"Ricky, you've gone absolutely swatty in the head," Rosie observed.

"Mario said I was a man," Rick said happily.

"Ricky, I always knew you were a man. Why do you think I love you?" She kissed him.

"That's cute," Irene observed. "First she kills him and now she kisses him."

"Why do you hate me?" Rosie asked her aunt.

"Rosie, your aunt doesn't hate you. In fact, she's here to save your hide," Mario explained.

"How's she going to do that?"

"She's going to talk to the beast."

"The beast?" Rick moaned. "You mean . . ."

"Shhhh . . ." Irene whispered.

Rosie was stunned at this news.

"Irene used to know the beast well," Mario explained.

"I thought the Caesares never had anything to do with the beasts," Rosie observed suspiciously.

"Irene wasn't a Caesare by birth. She was a Muncilli. She went to school with the beast. That's before she married Uncle Ignatius, God rest his soul." Hurriedly, Mario made the sign of the cross.

"But how can Aunt Irene help?" Rosie asked.

"Because your Aunt has a special relationship with the beast."

Irene giggled as she crossed her plump legs, patting the dimpled knees with affection. "We were engaged to be married," she announced proudly.

"W–h–a–t?" Rosie bellowed.

"Vito was mad for me. He wouldn't let me talk to any other boys. I had no brothers and my father was sick. So I thought I had to marry him. But Mario saved me."

"Mario?" Rick gushed.

"He knew that Iggie and I were madly in love. But Iggie wasn't strong the way Mario was. So Mario fought for the Caesare family honor."

"What happened?" Rosie asked.

"Your father went *mano a mano* with Vito Borgotta and won."

"Daddy!" Rosie said proudly. "You didn't?"

"Vito wasn't the beast he is now," her aunt continued. "But he was tough. And he's never forgiven your father."

"Is that why they're afraid of you?" Rosie asked Mario.

"Let's say they have respect," he observed.

"They know your father is a king among pigs," Irene boasted. "The name of Mario Caesare is spoken in whispers among men who admire courage."

"Wow!" Rick was impressed.

"I always kept the code of secrecy," Mario explained. "But you are breaking it. So if the beast moves against you, I have nothing to fight him with. Everyone is on his side."

"Not everyone," Irene said, uncrossing her legs and revealing, for a brief second, that she wore shocking-pink undies. Rick turned away quickly, ashamed at viewing Irene's inner sanctum. Then she waddled over to the wall mirror and fussed with her strawberry hair. She spit on two fingers, then turned and twisted her mane into tight curls. When she was through, she faced them, fluttering her false red eyelashes in Warner Brothers mid-Forties style. Aunt Irene often changed studios to suit her mood.

"I'm going to save your lives," she announced proudly.

"How can you do that?" Rick asked.

"Vito is still insane about me."

"But he was in love with Sally, and look at what happened to her," Rosie observed.

Irene shook her head violently. "No. Vito would never harm a woman he loved. That murder doesn't make sense."

"But if he didn't do it, then who did?" Rosie asked.

"That's what I intend to find out," Irene announced.

18

"Hey, don't worry about it," Irene said.

"The boss said to take care of you special," the body-guard announced. His eyes fastened on Rick, who was leaning as far back into the silk couch as he could, hoping he could fade into its gold-and-white-print brocade.

"I'm fine. Ricky, do you want something cold?"

"No, thank you, Aunt Irene."

Rick pronounced the word "aunt" very deliberately, hoping to impress upon the ghoulish bodyguard that he was related to an Italian and, thus, should not be killed. Rick's mind meandered. He knew that his father, the very autocratic Major Ramsey, had never contemplated that his one and only heir might lose his life in an Asbury Park, New Jersey, grand palazzo.

Certainly it was that. Irene hired a sleek gray limo to drive them to the place. "Here we are," she announced after two stressful hours on the road. Rick had taken a quick look out the window and had been startled. He couldn't believe that the beast's architectural masterpiece, which could board thirty-six guests, was really located in Asbury Park. It looked like it belonged in Venice, Italy, in another century.

The place was huge and built rectangularly, with shuttered windows dotting its surface. As the limo drove past the iron gate, Rick observed that the grounds were meticulously landscaped. The gate was operated by three men who looked like Italian Jimmy Cagneys. When the limo pulled up in front of the palazzo, Rick helped Aunt Irene out. As he held onto her, he began to tremble. What frightened Rick was the sight of the double doors encrusted with bronze figures, twelve in all. Carefully, he surveyed them, sensing that they must tell a tale. When he realized that the beast had engraved the birth of Christ in bronze on his entrance doors, Rick grimaced. That took balls.

"Some doors, eh, Rick?" Irene muttered, eyeing down the tall giant who was holding the main door open for them.

"They belong in a museum," Rick agreed.

The bronze figures should have prepared him for the interior of the house. In the center of the foyer was a three-tiered marble fountain. "Comes from a Venetian palace," Irene explained. The floors were also marble, probably from the finest Italian quarries. The long hall was dominated by several gold-leaf pillars, which held up the roof dome. Rick looked up. The entire dome looked like it belonged in a cathedral. Rick wondered where the beast had stolen the lovely mosaics that covered it. Beyond the fountain was an elegant circular staircase covered in white plush.

The bodyguard ushered them into an expansive grand salon where everything was gold. The drapes. The rugs. The couches. On the piano were photographs of family, all framed in gold. Next to the piano, the terrace doors opened onto a garden. Rick followed Irene outside, where the formal hedges were arranged in a classical manner. Beyond them, rows of trees formed elegant lanes. In the center of the garden was a wading pool of gray stone. "That used to belong to Napoleon," Irene pointed out. When they returned to the grand salon, a bodyguard ushered them into a smaller room. This petite salon was covered with velvet and silk. Green velvet drapes reminded Rick of *Gone With the Wind*. But these drapes were not fringed with thick gold tassles, as Miss Scarlet's had been. These drapes were dripping with rhinestones.

The floor was covered with wall-to-wall plush, the same shade of green. Everything was gilded gold, even the doorknobs.

Silently, Rick wondered whether his years at prep school had prepared him adequately for this elegance. Everything he looked at caused him severe visual shock. He sat down quickly, vowing not to reveal his trauma. Mario had requested that Rick be strong and stern in the face of the beast and his goons.

"Irene needs a man to escort her, kid," Mario explained after the visit had been arranged. "If I go along, the negotiation will sour."

"Negotiation?"

"Yes, the beast will get involved with me instead of her and nothing will work out. If you go with her, he will simply despise you, but he will feel secure enough to dismiss you as an enemy. That will give Irene the edge and she can work on him. Simple, huh?"

Rick was completely amazed at the intricate maze in which Mario dealt with life, liberty, and the pursuit of happiness.

"Are you sure you want to go?" Rosie asked. "This beast can be awful scary."

"Of course, I'll go," Rick volunteered, trying to control the panic in his throat.

"My hero," Rosie boasted to her family.

The adoring look in her eyes had gotten Rick through the ride down to Asbury Park, but now his nerves were failing. His legs began to buckle, but Irene, his companion, though older and of the female sex, was quite at ease when faced with the prospect of the beast's imminent appearance.

The bodyguard disappeared and a manservant wearing white knit gloves and a starched white cotton jacket buttoned up to his neck appeared. Rick felt sorry for the fellow. In this humidity, he must be choking. Then Rick realized that the temperature inside the house was quite comfortable. Probably an expensive air-conditioning unit was operating. The manservant bowed with formality. Rick shivered as two servants, dressed similarly, rolled out a tea cart. On it were elegant cream puffs and tea for three. When everything was ready, the master appeared.

The beast was wearing a dark blue satin robe trimmed with mink—even though it was summertime. He was slim, but his hands were huge and threatening. On his fingers he wore two rings. One was an immense ruby, the other a large emerald. Rick realized that the beast really did look like Paul Newman, even to the pure blue of his eyes.

The master of the house casually leaned on a statue of a large angel, which guarded the room.

"Irene, my darling. How are you?" he said, his arms opening wide to receive her.

"Vito, dear." Irene jumped up and walked over to the beast. Her glitter style looked even more tawdry against Vito's elegance. Rick guessed that the beast had to have a Milanese tailor, for the lines of the robe were flawless.

Irene gave the beast a Fellini kiss, a peck on each cheek. This kiss was popular with Italian women because it did not smear their lipstick and did not spread germs, since lips never touched. But the beast kissed Irene right smack on the lips. She glistened.

"Do you know my nephew, Rick Ramsey?"

"I've heard of him." Vito was annoyed because Rick was sitting down. "He's a writer, isn't he?"

Realizing Rick could not stand without trembling, Irene led the beast over to the couch.

"Let's sit," she said, patting a spot for Vito. "Rick and Rosie have been in love since they were kids. It's a Romeo and Juliet story."

"With a happier ending?" the beast questioned Irene.

"Oh, yes. They're very happy."

"Does your nephew speak?" he joked.

"Nice to meet you," Rick said, trying to sound calm so Mario would be proud of him.

But he wasn't calm. His legs felt like rubber. The back of his neck was pounding so loud that he had a hard time hearing. Every time he put his hand to his chest, his heart beat so rapidly he thought he was about to die. He felt nauseous, and pinpricks of tension climbed up and down his legs. And he had an erection. He placed his hands over his jacket opening, hoping the beast would not observe that overt fear produced sexual desire in WASP men.

"You have a wonderful family, Irene." The beast relaxed and leaned back on the couch, still eyeing Rick. "Unfortunately, I have no children."

"I don't, either," she said coyly.

"If we'd married, we would have had many."

"Life goes on," she said philosophically.

"But families make the world function. Especially for Italians. You know we are all anarchists. Put fifty Italians together in one room and they have different opinions about almost everything. We are the only individuals left in the world. That's why we need families. Without them, we have no strength. But with families, we rule!"

To make his point, he slammed his fist onto a marble table, looking like a monarch. Quickly, Rick looked around. He had the feeling there were more Italians in the room, but he could not spot them. Where were they hidden? He'd gotten good at spotting Italians. He knew they were around because a faint smell of garlic permeated the tea service.

"Would you like tea?" the beast asked Irene.

"Not right now." Instead, she rose and walked over to a large table where miniature soldiers were set in a battle plan. Vito followed her.

"Carthage, right?" she asked. He nodded. "But they attacked from this point." She corrected several miniatures.

"I see we still share the same passion for Rome," he said.

Then they began to move soldiers about and talk about the Roman battle of Carthage. From the couch, Rick was stumped. He'd known Irene for twenty years and assumed her only knowledge of Roman history was from *Ben Hur*— the movie, not the book. He quickly repeated his mantra: *Think Italian.* What are they really doing? What does it really mean?

"And those men were killed instantly," the beast said,

downing several Roman legions. "I am sorry." His eyes were glowing with winning. Irene suddenly placed several legions in another formation.

"And this is what happened here," she said, licking her plump lips.

Rick watched them watch each other. He knew that what was happening had nothing at all to do with the battle at Carthage. It had more to do with what was going to happen here, in this room. Perhaps he should take notes. He reached into a lapel pocket for a pad. Instantly, he was surrounded by two swarthy types who had apparently been hiding behind a large statue of the goddess Diana.

The beast turned, observing Rick. "Looking for something?"

"A pencil?" Rick's voice was shaky.

"Naw, you don't want a pencil," the beast said.

Quickly, the men frisked Rick. Then they took his pen and pencil. They nodded to Vito. Rick leaned back, saying a very long mantra he'd learned when he was married to Sharon and not having real sex. He whispered the chant for the entire time that Irene and the beast frisked about, playing at the battle of Carthage. Finally, it was over.

"You won." Irene congratulated him.

"You played well," he said.

They returned to the couch, hand in hand. Irene seemed pleased with the outcome of the battle because she began provocatively shaking her hips at Vito.

"Coffee?" he asked.

She nodded and he snapped his fingers. Three servants appeared carrying trays of cakes and espresso. With great formality, they set the trays on the marble table. Rick watched Irene serve in a most refined air. Sweat dripped from every pore of his body. He wondered who his aunt-in-law really was. He thought he had her pegged, but she was surprising him constantly.

After coffee, Irene began the real battle.

"Vito, I've come to talk to you about something important."

He laughed. "I didn't think you drove down to Asbury Park for coffee. I've invited you here many times, but you never leave Southampton." He looked at Rick. "Need a favor for him?"

"He's involved."

"Ask. You know I can't refuse you."

"It's about Sally . . ." she began.

Suddenly Vito's expression changed to unbearable sadness. Irene touched his hand.

"I know she meant a lot to you."

"I loved her."

Rick was startled by the beast's sincerity.

"What really happened?" Irene asked.

"We have an audience." Vito gestured to Rick.

"You can trust him."

Rick tried to look as trustworthy as possible.

"I had nothing to do with her death," Vito said.

"I knew it. I knew you could not harm her."

"I loved her too much."

"Was it business?" Irene asked.

He shook his head. "I am cursed," he muttered, running his hands through his sleek hair. "I was hurt that people could think I would harm one hair of Sally's head. My beautiful love." His blue eyes were stormy now. "Irene, you know how sincere I am?"

"You were always sincere," she agreed.

Carefully, Rick watched. Was this a beast? He was like everybody else. He had a heart. He hurt. He loved. Before Vito could speak again, a piercing scream filled the room. Rick jumped up too quickly. At once, he was surrounded by Vito's bodyguards.

"It's okay." Vito raised his hands and the men disappeared again.

"Filomena?" Irene asked.

"Yes."

"How is she?"

"The same."

"I'd like to see her."

"You wouldn't like it."

"We were best friends."

"Yes, when you dumped me, she was my consolation prize."

"But you love her."

"Yes, I do. Just as I love Sally, may she rest in peace." Quickly, he made the sign of the cross.

"You have a good heart, Vito."

"People don't understand that. They think I have no heart because of my business."

Suddenly, another piercing scream. Then footsteps and a nurse appeared.

"Your wife wants you, Don Vito," she said.

"Take care of her."

"She insists."

Rick watched as Vito's body caved in. It was as if the responsibility he had to bear in life was overwhelming him at this moment. This matter could not be delegated to inferiors. It was too important. He put his hand up to his forehead and rubbed it. He had hundreds of men impatient to perform anything he requested, but he had to do the most important things himself.

"You stay here," Vito said to Rick.

"Can't."

"Stay here."

"I'm ordered to stay with Aunt Irene."

"Whose orders?"

"Mario's," Irene confirmed.

"Do you always obey your father-in-law?" Vito asked Rick.

"I do when I'm acting for the family," Rick answered.

Irene smiled with pride.

"Okay, son." Then Vito asked Irene, "You sure he can be trusted?"

"He won't write about anything that happens here," she promised.

"How do I know that?"

"Because Mario would kill him."

He nodded at her logic. Rick wanted to shout, "I'm not a writer. I'm a nice guy who used to play football and I jog everyday and I married an obsessive, wonderful person who is an Italian and quite accidentally also a writer." But Rick knew that if he verbalized this, Vito would think less of him, Mario would cream him, and Rosie would hate him. So he remained silent. Besides, he knew this was very Italian. Italians liked silence while they manipulated fate.

Vito led Irene up the vast staircase. Rick followed, holding firmly to the banister. He prayed that he would not slip and fall. He watched Irene swinging her thick buttocks and the beast watching with an ecstatic look on his face. Rick was filled with admiration. This beast had enough guts to love passionately.

When they reached the top of the stairs, Vito turned down a long hall. Rick saw paintings from the thirteenth century on the walls. A fortune in art. Finally, they reached a room of many shades of pink. On a platform, a throne bed was covered with deep pink satin. The rugs were plush pink, and there were matching velvet drapes. Two couches of mauve pink stood in front of a pink marble fireplace. Lying on the plush rug, her head against the bed, was a woman in a pink silk negligee.

Her skin was flawless, as if a painter had decided to paint her portrait in pure porcelain. Her hair was spun gold, almost too perfect to be real. Her eyes were deep and a rare shade of black-brown. These mysterious eyes dominated her slim face with its high cheekbones and tantalizing lips. A delicate chain of diamonds encircled her graceful neck.

"Filomena." Irene quickly bent to speak to the woman.

When she saw Irene, the woman's eyes opened wide. She reached out. Irene stepped closer, but Vito interfered. "Don't get too close. She's dangerous."

"She won't hurt me."

"I'm afraid she would."

Protectively, Rick moved beside Irene.

"How long has she been this way?" Irene asked Vito.

"For a few years."

"Can the doctors help?"

"Her mind is almost gone."

Irene touched Vito's arm. "She was intelligent. She even went to college."

With this gesture, the woman came alive. Her nostrils flared, her mouth opened wide, and the screams that had chilled Rick before were repeated several times. She beat one arm against the bed. Then Rick saw why she was lying on the rug. Around her right wrist was a gold handcuff that kept her prisoner to the bed. Without thinking, Rick moved toward the woman.

"Don't touch her," Vito ordered.

"It's me, Filomena," Irene said. "Irene. I was your best friend."

"Bitch! Whore! Cunt!" From the elegant lips erupted a stream of obscenities, as one hand grasped the edge of Irene's skirt. Frightened, Irene turned away, but the woman would not let go. She pulled the skirt and Irene tripped, falling onto the rug beside Filomena. Filomena grabbed Irene by the throat. Irene screamed. Before Rick could move, Vito quickly pulled his wife's hands from Irene's throat. But Filomena was not afraid of Vito. Hissing, she drew his face to her with strong hands and kissed him passionately. Rick shuddered. It was like a vampire's kiss to draw blood. As she held onto Vito's lips, color left his face. He encircled her, drawn by her demonstration of obsessive passion.

The nurse appeared, carrying a hypodermic needle. Kneeling beside the woman, she plunged the needle deep into one arm. A few moments passed before she calmed, but Vito lay immersed in her arms until her insatiable lust disappeared. Then, Irene helped Vito to his feet. The nurse unlocked the handcuff, picked up Filomena, and without any help placed her in the center of the throne bed. Filomena's eyes were half-closed, but she watched Vito's every movement. When he recovered, he knelt beside her, taking her hand to his lips.

"Sleep, my darling," he whispered.

But she watched as he left the room. Then she began to

moan for him. Her moans followed them as they descended the stairs. In the salon, Irene sank into a chair.

"Aunt Irene, are you okay?" Rick asked.

"Ricky, it was bad."

"Can I get you anything?"

"I need to rest. Vito does too."

Vito sat down, his eyes half-closed.

"What's wrong with her?" Rick asked.

"Jealousy," Irene said simply. "She's always been crazy jealous of Vito. When they married, I couldn't go to the ceremony. She sent word that she would spit in my face if I turned up. I was her best friend, but she turned on me. She knew I loved Iggie, but Vito and I were once sweethearts, so she would never forgive me."

"Sad," Rick agreed.

"Vito," Irene said proudly, "will never abandon her. He knows how to love."

Rick watched Vito's expression and saw that Irene was right. The beast was still in love with the insane woman he'd married.

"Love doesn't stop when there's trouble. Or when someone is ill. Or even when they die," Irene said. "I still love Iggie, even though he's gone."

"I understand," Rick whispered.

Vito opened his eyes and looked at Irene fondly.

"So, Vito. Life is hard," she said, reaching out for his hand.

He waved his hands as if he were presenting a case to a jury. "I must have love. I cannot live without it."

19

A few days later, Anita Salerno phoned to say she was ready to give Rosie an interview. Rick and Rosie went to Anita's three-room apartment together, because Mario did not want Rosie to wander about SoHo without an escort.

"Would you like something to eat?" the petite woman asked. Anita had dark brown eyes that completely dominated her fragile face.

"No, thanks. Could we get to the interview?" Rosie asked in a businesslike manner.

She set out the tape recorder. Rick watched. Anita did not seem particularly anxious about the fact that every word was about to be recorded. Italians were strange, he thought. They wouldn't talk about important matters on the phone. They were constantly whispering in groups. They even had special nods and hand signs to convey information. But they seemed to have absolutely no problem about talking into a tape recorder. Maybe Rosie's thesis was correct. She maintained that all Italians were natural-born actors, and tape recorders encouraged their tendency to be always at center stage.

"Anita, you were going to tell us about Sally and Vito," Rosie encouraged.

As she spoke, Anita's dark eyes darted about the room.

Rick followed her gaze. Her eyes seemed to concentrate on an oil painting of the Madonna and Child, which hung on the living room wall.

"Sally was crazy mad for Vito," Anita stated. "Nothing else mattered to her. I warned her. I told her the neighborhood would label her a *mala femmina.*"

"What's that?" Rick asked.

Rosie shot him a nasty look for breaking into Anita's confession.

"It means a woman who is not a good woman," Anita explained calmly. "But, I wasn't prepared for how the neighborhood feels about Sally now. After all, she was a good wife and mother. One mistake and they call her a *puttana.* May God rest her soul." Anita made the sign of the cross quickly.

"What's—" Rick began.

"It means whore," Rosie explained angrily.

"In our families, the woman is the center," Anita said ceremoniously. "If she acts *disgraziato,* then what happens to her family?"

"Did her husband know?" Rosie relentlessly pursued the truth.

"I don't think so. But everyone else did. My husband is Tony's brother. I said to him, 'Frank, listen, you can't tell Tony. He'll kill Sally and then what will happen to Angelique? She'll be an orphan.' But it happened anyway."

From the end table, she grabbed a large framed photograph of a beautiful girl, about thirteen, with long blond hair and soft gray eyes. Rick stared at the photograph. He'd seen that face before.

"She doesn't look like Sally," Rosie observed.

"She looks like Tony's mother. See." Anita pointed to a small miniature of a woman in an old-fashioned dress.

"Is she still alive?" Rick asked, certain that he'd seen the woman walking in SoHo.

"No. She died in Italy a few years ago."

"Had she ever come here?"

"No, she wouldn't leave Italy."

Rick was puzzled. He'd seen this face somewhere.

"So, Tony didn't know about the affair?" Rosie asked.

"Sally didn't want to hurt Tony. That's how she got into this mess. Vito threatened to harm her family."

Rosie nodded.

"Who could predict that Sally would fall for him?" Anita twisted the folds of her dress, looked up at Rosie and shrugged. As Rosie waited in silence, Rick took notes on the apartment. It was only three rooms. The small living room had one couch, two armchairs, and a color TV. From his seat, Rick could see into another room, probably a bedroom. Two posters of the dancer Isadora Duncan were taped on the door.

"Is Angelique living with you?" Rosie asked Anita.

"Yes." Anita pointed to the smaller room. "She wants to be a dancer. Did you know that Sally took her to that ballet school on University Place when she was only five years old?"

"Will we have a chance to meet her?" Rosie asked.

"She should be home any minute."

"Anita, have you had contact with Vito?"

Anita looked concerned. "Yes, that's one of the reasons I decided to talk to you."

Rosie's eyes glinted with interest.

"I know Don Vito did not harm Sally. He was too much in love with her to do that. But Sally is dead. *Che sera sera*," Anita said sadly. "But Vito has been coming here to visit. And I don't know why."

"Why do you think?"

"I don't know," she repeated in a worried tone. "He doesn't talk about Sally."

"What does he do?"

"He sits and has coffee. He likes to bring presents to Angelique."

"What kind of presents?"

"A gold chain. And ballet books." She pointed to a big pile of books in a corner. "Things like that. Expensive things. I guess he feels bad about the girl losing her mother and father."

"Is your husband here when . . ." Rosie began.

"Of course," Anita broke in adamantly. "I wouldn't let

Vito visit without Frank here. But," she said nervously, "it's got me worried."

"Worried?" Rick echoed.

"What does he want from us?" Anita questioned.

"What do you think?" Rosie repeated.

"I'm not sure . . ."

At that moment, a young girl walked into the apartment. Her hair was brushed back into a ponytail and carefully pinned with fresh flowers. She wore a thin gold chain around her neck, which was too glamourous for the jeans and T-shirt she wore. She was wholesome-looking, unusually healthy for a child of the city. Her sweet smile lit up her beautiful face as she walked gracefully toward them. Rick smiled. The girl reminded him of Rosie at that age.

"Angelique, come here," her aunt said sternly. "How was your class?"

"Wonderful, but hot," she replied. "I need to shower."

"Say hello to Mr. and Mrs. Ramsey first."

"Hi ya," she nodded.

"Hello," Rosie said.

"You're going to be a dancer?" Rick asked.

Now the radiance on her face was dazzling and Rick felt overcome with admiration for her.

"You bet," she said. "Excuse me."

"What were you saying?" Rosie prodded Anita after Angelique had shut the door to her room.

"Turn that thing off," Anita ordered. "Can't talk with her here."

"Can we continue tomorrow?"

"Let me call you. Okay?"

Rick could tell Rosie did not like that much.

"Thank you very much," he said to Anita.

"So, we'll hear from you soon?" Rosie pressed hard.

"In a few days," Anita agreed, as she ushered them out of the apartment.

They raced down the three flights of stairs to the street, where Rick stopped quickly.

"Rosie. We've got to find your father."

"For heaven's sake, why?"

"Because I've had an Italian insight."

She shrugged her shoulders. "Stop kidding around," she ordered.

"I'm not kidding around. Remember when I told you that Vito said that he absolutely had to have love in his life?"

"What are you getting at?"

"That means he needs somebody new to love. After all, Sally is dead and Filomena is whacko."

"So what?" she screamed impatiently.

"Will you keep it down?" Rick scolded. "Well, he's been coming around to visit Anita and Frank, hasn't he?"

"Yes. That's what Anita told us."

"And he's been bringing Angelique gifts."

"Uh-huh."

Suddenly, Rosie's eyes flew open. "Oh, no," she screamed.

"Oh, yes," Rick confirmed.

"You mean he's after Angelique? But she's only thirteen."

"You told me that girls her age get married in Sicily."

"That's true. Ohhhhh, Rick."

"Wait, there's more."

"What else? Come on, tell me."

"Do you know whom Angelique looks like?"

"Her grandmother in Italy."

Rick shook his head. "Someone else," he said.

"Who?" She began jumping up and down, which caused a lot of attention because her free breasts were bobbing nicely.

"Stop that," Rick ordered, noticing his wife was the focus of male glances.

"Tell me. Tell me."

"Angelique looks like Filomena Borgotta."

"No?"

"That's what was bugging me. I knew I'd seen that face before. Angelique's a young version of Mrs. Beast!"

20

The teenager hunched over the church pew, her long hair covering bare shoulders. The night was very hot, and though she was in church, Angelique wore a tissue-thin cotton top held up with spaghetti straps. Underneath, she wore no bra.

Watching, the slim woman could see the outline of the girl's budding breasts.

Angelique bowed her head low before the elaborate altar. The church was in semi-darkness after evening service, but many candles glowed and the city's sunset shone through the church's stained-glass dome. The elaborate altar had three sections. To the left was a small altar devoted to the Madonna and Child, where Angelique prayed. Her eyes reflected anguish as she whispered prayers. Finally she sobbed. Then she muffled the sounds with her hands.

The slim woman watched, hidden by the black cloth of the confessional. This cloth was to protect the confessor from exposure as sins were confessed to a priest. The woman remembered her childhood days when she went to confession. She liked the darkness, where she shared her inner thoughts with an anonymous priest. But no more of that. Now she shared herself only with her man. There was no need for anyone else. Not even God.

Emotionally, she vowed fidelity to her love. But he was a man and men had roving eyes. When he'd visited Angelique at first, she'd thought it was simply business. But she feared now that it was more than that. She watched the teenager at the altar. Her innocence was obvious. The girl was as beautiful as her mother had been, though in a different way. Sally had the beauty of Southern Sicily. Angelique reflected the beauty of the North of Italy.

The woman knew she could not compete. The girl was too young. Her freshness, her untouched body, her trusting eyes—all marks of a virgin. Men adored that look. An older woman could never duplicate it, no matter how fit she was. Men were silly creatures. After they cultivated a woman's love, they turned to inexperienced girls.

Angelique wiped her beautiful eyes with a Kleenex. Then she genuflected before the altar and walked up the side aisle. The woman in the confessional opened her alligator bag. She took out the cord and wove it around her fists tightly. She listened as the girl's footsteps came closer.

Suddenly, there was a flurry of voices.

The woman pulled on the cord, hurting herself. Then she heard Angelique passing by the confessional. The woman steeled herself as nausea overcame her. She'd wanted to feel the cord around the girl's throat, wanted to see her gasp for life, wanted to see her turn ugly. But it was too dangerous. She put the cord back into her bag. The voices grew dimmer. She pulled back the black curtain and hurried out of the church.

As she drove from the city, she comforted herself. There was nothing to worry about. After all, she was not a professional and it took her longer to succeed.

But succeed she would. Yes, there would be another opportunity to get rid of Angelique.

21

"Kid. You are coming along. I may even retire as head of the family soon."

"Mario, please be serious."

"I am being serious. You're a contender, kid."

"We've got to save Angelique from Vito's lust," Rosie interrupted.

Her father's eyes popped. He called out to his wife, who was, as usual, bending over the stove.

"Celia, am I kidding around?"

"No."

"Celia, tell my daughter and son-in-law that I think this is serious."

Celia turned away from the meatballs she was frying. "Your father thinks this is serious."

"Celia, tell the kid he's doing fine. I'm glad I decided to groom him. Everybody said Rick would never make it." Happily, Mario scratched his unshaven cheeks. "But he's thinking Italian and he isn't even forty yet."

"Ricky, Mario thinks you're doing fine," Celia uttered solemnly.

The Caesare kitchen was filled with bright sunlight. Rick leaned against the windowsill, looking out to SoHo's backyards. Long clotheslines testified that Italians did not believe in electric dryers. He examined the inventory of men's shirts and women's blouses. There was no underwear. Italians felt undies should be privately dried. Rick turned, facing his father-in-law.

"Mario, we've got to do something," he said seriously.

"Of course, we're going to do something. But first eat something."

"Dad, we don't have time to eat," Rosie said. "Look, I've got an idea. Remember what the Jews did when the Nazis marched into Holland?"

"What have the Nazis got to do with Vito's lust?" Celia asked. As she spoke, the hot oil from the frying pan spit on her face. She wiped her face clean.

"I know about lust," Mario announced. "It can kill a man."

"You've never felt real lust in your life," his wife pronounced as she spooned the large meatballs onto a platter. "Good men don't lust."

"We could send Angelique to her cousins in Sicily," Mario said, concentrating on the thick meatballs. Nearby a large pot simmered with fresh tomatoes and a number of spices. The meatballs would be added to Celia's famous Bolognese sauce, which she'd learned to cook when she was five.

"Can't I have one?" Mario asked timidly. Though he was a lion in the streets and a better chef than Celia, Mario always allowed his wife to dominate in the kitchen. He felt this was responsible for their happy marriage.

"Can't you wait?" Celia asked impatiently.

"There are two things in life I can't wait for," he replied.

"And what are they?" Celia laughed, knowing the answer.

"Meatballs," he replied. "And love."

"Well, you can have the meatballs," she announced and spooned two large meatballs onto a plate, handing him a knife and fork also.

"Dad, will you please pay attention," Rosie complained, rocking the chair she sat on until it squeaked.

"Stop that," her mother ordered.

"Wait a sec," Mario said gruffly as he cut one meatball in half, forked it, and offered it to Rosie. She shook her head. He offered it to Rick.

"No, thanks," Rick said.

"Eat it. I know you'll like it," Celia said.

"Okay."

Timidly, he chewed the meatball. Rosie threw Rick a hateful look. This was the week they were to eat nothing but greens in an attempt to slim down for television appearances.

"You broke our diet," she complained.

"Magnifico!" Mario kissed his hands and waved them happily in the air. "Okay, now to business. What about the Nazis?"

"When the Nazis entered Holland, remember Anne Frank and her family hid in an attic," Rosie explained.

"Nobody has an attic in SoHo," Rick observed.

"True. But Aunt Irene has all those loft buildings. She's always remodeling the lofts. Why can't Angelique hide in one of them?" Rosie asked.

"Because," Mario explained, "the beast will find out. Our family is the first family he'll watch if Angelique disappears."

"Besides," Celia observed, "Aunt Irene would never be able to lie to the beast."

"Why not?" Rosie asked.

"She can negotiate, but she can't lie," Mario explained cautiously. "If she's caught in a lie, all her clout with him evaporates. Remember that, Rick."

Rick was startled. His Italian education hadn't even really begun. He had much to learn. There were many complications, twists and turns, to living the Italian way. Rick wondered whether he'd be able to master it all. In his spare time, he was reading the dialogues of Machiavelli. Now he realized why the Western World was insipid. They'd taken Machiavelli's theories to heart, but weakened his thesis with additions of honesty, integrity, and the most irresponsible attitude of all: never being caught. What was it that J. R. Ewing always said on Mario's favorite television show, 'Dallas'? "Once you give up integrity, the rest is easy." J.R. could very easily be Italian. If he changed his cowboy suits and boots for Giorgio Armani and Gucci, he'd pass.

"We've got to have a plan," Rosie insisted. "Rick, stop looking out the window."

155

"What about an underground?" Celia asked, spooning the thick meatballs into the sauce. "Remember that movie with Tyrone Power and the French woman he married? The one with the short hair like a man's?"

"Annabella," Rick observed. Rosie looked startled. Her mother never had any fresh ideas.

"Remember the way they moved those people around in cellars and kitchens?" Celia continued.

"That's a good idea," Rosie admitted.

Celia put the cover on the sauce. Then she sat at the table with the rest of the family.

"So your mother has brains after all?" She challenged Rosie.

"Can we do it, Dad? Can we organize an underground? And whom can we trust?"

"I'll tell you how we'll do it," he announced. "The beast is Sicilian. Right?"

"Right," everyone answered in unison.

"And who hates Sicilians more than anyone?"

"Who?" Rick asked.

"The Calabrese, that's who," Rosie announced.

"Right," Mario agreed. "Our family is Calabrese and we hate those damn Sicilians." He smiled, picking his teeth with a gold toothpick that Aunt Irene had given him on his last birthday. "What we've got to do is contact all the Calabrese families. We've got to send a message around that we all have to help this child. But," he added cautiously, "our family has to stay out of it because the beast will come to us first."

"But will the Calabrese really go against the beast?" Rick asked.

"The Calabrese are very strong," Rosie said with pride.

"They'll go against the beast because this involves Angelique's virginity. It's her most precious possession, remember." Mario threw a nasty look at Rosie. "Of course, in America some girls don't agree with this. My daughter didn't believe in virginity and white wedding gowns."

"Don't bring that up again," Rosie protested. "Besides, I wore a white wedding gown at my wedding."

"Yeah, but . . ." Celia began, but Rosie shot her a nasty look.

"Thank God," said Mario, "there is only one man in your life. I said to God, 'Look, my daughter can't help herself. She's modern.' When you left the family to live in sin with Rick, I thought I'd never show my face in the neighborhood again." He put down the gold toothpick and began cleaning it with a napkin. "But God was good to me. The kid came through and married you."

Rick's chest began to swell, but Rosie shot him a *be careful* look. Her father had never learned about the life she led after Rick married Sharon.

"And he's beginning to know the score." Mario looked at Rick with pride.

"Dad, can we get back to Angelique?" Rosie said. "You don't have it straight. It's not her virginity we're saving."

"You bet it is," Mario insisted.

"No, it's not."

"Then what is it?" Celia asked.

"We're saving her from rape!"

Celia jumped up, banging her fist on the table. "Watch your filthy mouth," she warned. "You're in my house, remember?" She rushed over to the stove. "You've spoiled the sauce."

"It's okay," Rosie observed.

"You know everything has to be quiet when the sauce is simmering. I taught you that when you were six."

"Five," Rosie corrected.

"Six. And you still don't know how to cook. Poor Ricky has to eat in restaurants all the time, don't you, Ricky?"

"Mother, we eat health food," Rosie announced. "It's not hard to cook fresh greens."

"You're turning into rabbits," Celia said with contempt. "Look how skinny you're getting."

"We have to be thin for television. It adds ten pounds."

"Who's on television?"

"We're going to be on television when the book comes out."

Celia put her hands through her hair and began tearing

at the strands. *"Madonna mia,"* she screamed. "My daughter is insane. We're all going to get murdered in our beds."

"Calm down, Celia," Mario ordered.

At once, Celia put her hands over her mouth and began gasping for breath. Rick ran to the sink, filled a glass with tap water, and handed it to her.

"You're a good boy," she gasped. "My daughter doesn't know how lucky she is." She grabbed his hand. "Ricky, you're not going on television, are you?"

Rick nodded sheepishly.

"Oh, you too," she moaned.

"Can we get back to the problem at hand?" Rosie asked officiously. "Dad, can we really set up a hideout with the Calabrese?"

"Sure."

"How do we do it?" Rick asked.

"We go to the women. Calabrese women are the best. You're married to one," Mario boasted to Rick. "Those women would stand up against the beast for the sake of that young girl. We'll contact all the Calabrese women in Manhattan and tell them our problem. I'll bet before the day is over, we'll have more volunteers than we can count."

As usual, he was correct. *Keep Angelique Salerno from Don Vito's lust* became the password in SoHo circles. Before evening, the young girl was shipped to Rosanna Armano's six-room apartment on East 66th Street. Angelique was told that she would be safer uptown until her parents' murderers were found. After she left the Salerno apartment, the chase began. The next morning, two long dark limos imposed themselves on SoHo's side streets. Like poisonous snakes, they staked out Angelique's school. But they were foiled. The priests, knowing the poor girl's plight, had allowed her to attend classes at a Catholic school on the Upper East Side. Mario estimated that Vito would never search uptown because it was Fat Johnny Pesto's territory. Vito's presence might be taken as a challenge to Fat Johnny's terrain.

Of course, Vito made a thorough search of SoHo. Each morning, SoHo residents who happened to be Italian were asked to open their doors. Everything was done with politeness, and Vito promised that no one would get hurt or killed. Stuttering housewives were faced with tall dark men who searched everywhere. Vito was organized. Block by block he combed SoHo for Angelique. But she was nowhere to be found. *Vito's lust* became the talk of the neighborhood. At three P.M. mothers met their children at school to usher them safely home. Older women, dressed in traditional black, attended church services; afterwards they hung around on the church's steps, vowing to defend Angelique. Stories were circulating about how Vito's goons had actually knocked on artists' doors, pretending to be collecting for Catholic Charities. Vito must be going crackers. How could he think that the Italians would let SoHo artists protect Angelique? Fists were raised and lips curled among the female population of Italian SoHo. Women who would spit at the word *feminist* were organizing to challenge the beast's autonomy. *Save Angelique's virginity* was the whispered phrase at vegetable markets, where women volunteered to other women the fact that the broccoli rabe did not look green and therefore would be bitter to the taste. At the pastafresha store, women ordered fresh ravioli and fettucini as they whispered about the plight of their sex when faced with male lust. The challenge of saving Angelique's virginity became the main drama of SoHo, replacing food as the topic of all Italian conversations.

Rick was treated as a hero. As he jogged along SoHo streets in his never-ending search for action (according to Mario), women smiled at him. Plump women. Thin women. Old women. Young women. Many with mustaches. All patted him on the back because it was known that he had figured out the beast's lust. And he wasn't even Italian! They nodded to one another that he had been reared with them, lived with them, cohabitated with one of their princesses and married her, so he was practically Italian. If only he could forget the fact that he was born in Connecticut, that strange place somewhere to the north of New York City.

The days flew by quickly. On the weekend, Rick received an urgent phone call from Mario to meet him at the club.

"Can I come in my jogging shorts?" Rick asked.

"Cover your legs" was Mario's response.

A half-hour later, Rick stood outside Mario's club, a storefront painted black so that pedestrians could not know what went on inside. Rick knocked. Crazy Nuz, who owned the corner grocery store, opened the door. Rick walked into a room where six tables were set up. Seated at the tables were men wearing hats and playing cards. Since it was lunchtime, several munched on sandwiches and sipped espresso.

"I'm here to see Mario," Rick said to Nuz.

"How are you, kid?"

Rick smiled graciously. He liked being a hero.

"Mario's in the back." Crazy Nuz pointed to a private alcove.

Rick's father-in-law was dressed formally in a white shirt, light blue tie, and light blue sharkskin suit. He stared at Rick's uncovered legs and frowned.

"You're late," he complained.

"The postman stopped me," Rick apologized. "Guess what was in the mail?"

Mario shrugged his shoulders.

"Our book contract. When we sign it, we'll get our check."

"You won't get happy writing books," Mario said gruffly. "Besides, you won't be able to live in the neighborhood if you write it. If the beast doesn't get you, someone else will."

Nuz stood at the table rubbing his hands together.

"You want a sandwich, kid?" he asked. "And coffee?"

"Yes."

"I got this machine that takes thirty minutes to heat up. But when it's ready, I make it sing. The coffee is great. Can you wait thirty minutes, kid?"

"Okay."

"No one talks about the beasts," Mario said glumly when they were alone.

"The kid came through, huh, Mario?" A huge man stopped at the table. "You and Rosie must be very proud." He patted Mario on the back. Mario smiled. "You're all right, kid," the man said before he left.

"You see that," Mario said. "Everybody knows about you and Rosie. You've got to stop her from writing that book."

"She's home right now writing a new chapter, which she calls 'The Beast's Lust.'"

Mario's face turned beet red and his cheeks began to puff. "Jesus. She's gonna get you both killed," he said.

"There isn't any way I can convince her to give this up. She's determined to get to Hollywood."

"So what's out there?" He raised his fist to Rick. "It's crapola. I don't know how Frank stands it."

"Frank?"

"Sinatra, dumbo."

Nuz appeared with a large tray of hero sandwiches filled with spicy salami, provolone, pepperoni, and green peppers. When Rick bit into one, Nuz smiled widely.

"What an appetite he has. Your daughter is lucky," he said to Mario. "I'll bring the coffee as soon as the machine sings."

Rick chomped on the spicy stuff, knowing it would upset his stomach.

"Mario," he said, between chomps, "what's your murder theory?"

"Shhhhh." Mario put his finger to his lips. "You gotta lower your voice."

"But this is your private club."

"You can't trust no one."

"All right," Rick grumbled.

Mario whispered, "Do you know about Gelenta?"

"What's Gelenta?"

"It's a town on the coast of Sicily. It seems they have a custom there that when they want revenge, they cut off a hand of someone who's alive. Then they take the hand and hide it. They believe that whoever finds the severed hand is cursed forever."

Rick's stomach began reacting badly to this dramatic bit of information, but Mario continued. "In Gelenta, people who walk around without their right hands are spit on and people throw stones at them. Everybody knows why they don't have

161

two hands. But here, in America, Sicilians don't follow these customs. That's why the murderer killed Sally and Tony after he cut their hands off. If the victims lived in Sicily, they'd still be alive."

"Some life without a hand."

"It's not bad. You can do most things. You can eat. You can make love. Anyhow, kid, what I wanted you to know is that Vito's wife comes from Gelenta."

"Jesus! Do you think she did it?"

"Naw. A woman couldn't do this kind of thing. You saw Filomena. She's crazy. Anyhow Vito's got her handcuffed to her bed. But she has male cousins in Sicily. Maybe they did it for her—"

Suddenly Mario jumped to his feet. His bearing was like a Roman commander in battle. "Who let you in here?" he asked in a threatening tone of voice.

Rick looked around and was astonished to see Detective Arthur Kushel, wearing a safari summer suit.

"Hello, Mr. Ramsey," Kushel said.

Rick barely nodded, wondering whether there were machine guns behind the espresso machine, and whether he would be in the line of fire.

"Mr. Caesare, if you don't mind, I'd like to talk to your son-in-law."

"I do mind. Lithuanians are not allowed inside this club."

Kushel reached into his breast pocket for his badge. Rick looked around. The door to the club was half opened and two beefy types guarded the entrance.

"Do I have to teach you good manners again?" Mario threatened.

"Mr. Ramsey. I'm looking for Angelique Salerno. I understand you know where the girl is?" Kushel asked.

Rick shook his head no.

"Well, I've had a tip—" Kushel began.

"Tip, my ass. You're a ballbuster," Mario shouted. The two beefy types looked in, but Kushel waved them away.

"I know that the girl has been moved to another location because of a certain party's interest in her."

"What is this world coming to?" Mario asked the men in dark hats, who had stopped playing cards and were watching Kushel with intensity.

"I know you've become the caretaker of that child." Kushel smiled at Rick, revealing that his teeth had many cracks. Rick wondered whether the cracks came from tuna fish, as Rosie often warned.

"Look, I told you," Mario threatened, "my son-in-law is off-limits unless you have a charge against him."

"As a good citizen, I know Mr. Ramsey would like to help the police," Kushel said.

"I . . ." Rick began, but Mario threw him a dread look.

"Lithuanian," Mario said to Kushel, "you're not welcome here."

"I'm sorry you feel that way, Mr. Caesare. I came in friendship."

"I pick my friends," Mario said quickly. "And I'm very choosy. Beat it, why don't you?"

Rick waited for Kushel to arrest Mario for being rude, but instead, the Lithuanian cowered when faced with Mario's fury. Rick was stunned. How did Mario know when and how to bend the fates to his advantage?

"Look, Mr. Caesare, we're going to find the girl. We have a tail on your son-in-law. He won't be able to take a crap without our knowing it."

"Get out."

"Sooner or later—" Kushel continued.

Suddenly, every man in the room rose to his feet and began walking toward Kushel. All had their right hands in their pockets. Kushel turned. Quickly, he left.

"Shut the door," Mario shouted to Nuz.

"I'm sorry. I left it open because the machine's singing made everything so hot," Nuz apologized, hurriedly shutting the door.

"Don't let it happen again," Mario ordered. "Kid, don't let that Lithuanian dick bother you."

22

"Christ. I hope none of our friends see us, Rick."

They were a sleazy vision in black-leather motorcycle motif. Punk style. Clingy leather pants. Spikey shoes with matching belt. A black and silver T-shirt with the letters spelling PUNK IS SEXY. On her head, Rosie wore a platinum-colored Mohawk wig. Its sideburns were bright orange streaks, which clashed with the midnight-blue makeup darkening her face. Her ears were stuck with silver safety-pin earrings. Rick hated wigs, so he hid his hair under a black-leather cap. They were pure punk, not an unusual sight in SoHo, but very noticeable on East 66th Street.

"Did you see that?" Rosie laughed as a pedestrian did a full turn at the sight of her swaggering leather buttocks. Rick tried not to react. After all, they were in disguise for a good cause. He squirmed in the tight leather pants. The weather was too hot for leather, but punk was the only disguise they could manage on such fast notice.

It had happened early this morning. The 7 A.M. phone call from Angelique had disturbed Rick, who was just getting into his deep dream cycle.

"Rick, it's Angelique," the soft voice had announced.

He jumped up at once, waking up Rosie. "Are you all right?" he asked.

"Is she all right?" Rosie asked him.

"I'm fine," the girl said.

"Are you sure?" Rosie insisted, grabbing the phone from Rick.

"Yes, absolutely. The only thing is that I've got to go down to ballet school today."

"Absolutely impossible," Rosie said.

"Mario said to stay uptown," Rick warned on the bathroom extension. Angelique's early call had frightened him, so his bladder needed to be attended to.

"But I can't. I've been uptown for a week and I'm going bananas. I can't get my mind turned on," the girl complained.

"Angelique," Rosie said harshly. "You must keep a low profile right now. If Vito finds you, we'll never see you again."

"But, Rosie, I'm supposed to dance the part of the princess in our annual concert. It's this afternoon and all the kids are depending on me."

"Let me call you back," Rosie said.

In the kitchen, Rick ground fresh coffee beans as Rosie paced.

"What time is it?" he asked sleepily.

"Seven A.M."

"My God, let's make love. It's too early to work."

"No, darling. We have to help Angelique. The poor kid. Look at what she's been through in the last months. Her parents were found dead on a roof—without their hands. The next thing, she's shipped off to Sixty-Sixth Street without any of her friends. You know how SoHo people get when they're not in SoHo. They freak out. I'd say that Angelique is being pretty good about all of this."

"Little Mother." He kissed her. "You're really worried, aren't you?"

Rosie's eyes were concerned. "Guess so. She needs someone to look after her. Let's think of some way she can dance at the concert. It's important to her."

"Simple," Rick said. "We'll go in disguise."

"Oh, Rick. You're a genius."

That's when Rick thought about the Pain Shop, which was located three doors away. The shop had been open for a year. At first, it was tiny and grimy, but pain was popular, so the shop immediately caught on. Now it was done up in lucite and steel. After breakfast, Rick and Rosie ran down to the shop and asked the owner, Montana Smiley, to disguise them. Montana agreed. When they left the shop, even Mario wouldn't recognize them. And they had an outfit for Angelique, too, which Rick was carrying in a shopping bag with the words PAIN IS FUN.

They took many precautions on their way uptown. They rode the A train to 86th Street and hopped on the crosstown bus to Lexington Avenue. There, they jumped on the Lexington Avenue downtown to Hunter College. If a beast had been able to follow them through the maze of subway riders, Rick would have to congratulate him.

Quickly, they found Rosanna Armano's building. Two middle-aged women frowned as Rick and Rosie walked into the lobby. They watched warily as Rick rang the bell with a prearranged signal. Three short rings. Four long rings. Then they ran up the four flights of stairs to Rosanna's apartment.

The plump woman stood in the doorway holding a heavy frying pan. Her gray eyes blinked over her spectacles.

"Who's this?" she asked.

Though the bell signal had been prearranged, Rosie knew that the punk disguise would frighten Rosanna. She pulled off the Mohawk wig and her Italian curls fell about her strangely distorted face.

"I'm in disguise. It's Rosie."

"Don't look like Rosie." The woman folded her arms across her chest firmly, still holding on to the heavy pan.

"Honest, it's me. And it's Rick."

Rosanna shook her head no.

"Say something in Italian," Rick suggested.

"The beasts know Italian," Rosie scolded.

"Say something in Calabrese."

"I don't know Calabrese."

The woman's eyes darted from one face to the other, searching for something familiar.

"What's your grandmother's maiden name?" she asked suddenly.

"Wadsworth," Rick answered quickly.

"What?" she shouted.

"Silly, she means me," Rosie said. "It's Placerno."

One of the facts of Italian family life was that the children learned their family tree at a pre-school age so that facts could be checked during emergencies like this.

The woman suddenly put the pan down and opened the door.

"I haven't seen you in so long." She kissed Rosie on both cheeks soundly. "You look miserable."

"Sorry. It's a disguise. It was the only one we could get in a hurry."

"They won't recognize you looking like two gooks," the older woman agreed.

"Where's Angelique?" Rosie asked when they entered the neat plant-filled apartment.

"Here I am." The girl was wearing a sky-blue ballet leotard. "Come on. We're going to be late."

"Wait a sec. Honey, you've got to get into this outfit," Rick said, handing the shopping bag to the girl.

Angelique looked into it. "Ugh," she said. "No way."

"Honey," Rick said sternly, "this is the only way we can take you downtown. And we really shouldn't be doing this at all. If Mario knew we were even thinking about it, he'd have a fit."

Rosie nodded in agreement.

"But University Place is not SoHo," Angelique protested.

"It's only across the park," Rosie said. "Do what Rick says."

"I'll look like a mug."

"Only until we reach the school. Then you can change. Honest," Rosie promised.

"All right." She disappeared into the bedroom. When she appeared a few seconds later, she was wearing an orange wig, a flared short leather skirt, and a vest that was too tight.

"You look like animals," Rosanna observed calmly.

"We'll bring her right back after the concert," Rick promised.

"I'll make ravioli," the older woman said. "You'll stay for dinner."

"See you."

Downstairs, they grouped themselves into a Three Musketeers formation. Arms wound about each other, they hopped onto the downtown Lexington Avenue express. As usual, the subway car was jammed with pushers, hustlers, junkies, and suburbanites, all staring at the punk trio with great distaste. Apache Punk was an accepted way of life in SoHo and points southeast, but uptown it was considered vile.

When they reached Union Square, they ran up to the street and tried to avoid the constant stream of muggers. They turned down University Place, where the street became sane and sensible. Quickly, they sped past the elegant antique warehouses, the chic Mexican restaurants, and the new Pasta Gardens. They reached Washington Place, which was mobbed. Across the street, the park had become an informal campus for the university. Students scurried about in groups, carrying books and parcels. Groups of pushers called out prices. The trio turned onto a side street where Angelique's ballet school was located. Inside, a stern-faced woman greeted them.

"Yes? What do you want?"

"It's me, Mrs. Reasoner. Angelique."

"Why are you dressed that way?"

"We've been making a film," Rick stuttered.

"You're very late. We didn't know what to do." Mrs. Reasoner pouted.

"I'm here now. Should I go in?"

"By all means. But take that awful costume off. Do you have your ballet things?"

"Yes, M'am."

"Good." She turned to Rick and Rosie. "Could you wait outside, please."

"How long will the program last?" Rosie asked.

"About an hour."

Downstairs, Rosie asked, "Want to hang out in the park, Ricky?"

"What are we going to do for the next hour?"

"We can take notes on the environment for our book."

"I'd rather neck."

Holding hands, they entered the northeast end of the park and sat on a bench. Nearby, a slim woman was lying on the grass, putting long, thin acupuncture needles into her face. Each time a needle went into her flesh, she moaned with pain. A young man with cropped hair observed her. Each time she gasped, he'd strum his guitar.

"New Wave," Rosie observed.

The woman exposed her left breast and began delicately placing needles into it. The moans grew louder and so did the guitar sounds. Then she began shrieking and the young man plugged into his portable electronic equipment to match the sounds. Rick looked carefully at the woman's breast. Her nipple was covered with a strip of black electrical tape.

"I wonder whether her nipple and the equipment are connected?" he said.

"You gone nuts?" Rosie asked.

Then the woman exposed her right breast and the same process of needle puncture began. The shrieks grew louder and so did the guitar. Two policemen noticed them and stopped to observe the scene. Then students began clamoring about, laughing and talking.

"We'd better cool out," Rosie whispered. "Let's become part of the scene," she teased as she placed her legs on Rick's lap.

"Mmmmm," Rick moaned. Black-leather pants were strangely exciting. "Touch me, honey."

"We'll get arrested."

"We've been arrested before."

"No, we haven't."

"Besides, sitting next to an exposed woman with needles in her breasts is a good cover," he protested.

"Well . . . maybe . . ." she agreed.

Discreetly, Rosie snuggled her hand under Rick's leather shirt.

"Remember when we used to pet in the doorway of your house?" he asked.

"Uh-huh," she hissed.

"Remember how you wanted to give up your virginity?"

"Yes, but you refused. You said I had to stay a virgin until I was sixteen. Why did you do that?"

"Because of Mario," he answered swiftly. "He would have killed me."

"But he would have killed you anyway, after I was sixteen. Why sixteen?"

"It seemed moral, somehow."

"You people from Connecticut are really strange."

"I always wondered how you could go against your family. They swore you had to be a virgin until you married."

"You turned me on, darling. I fell madly in love with you."

"Sweet thing," he murmured.

Three junkies passed by and spotted the naked needled woman lying on the grass. As her accompanying guitar swain played, the junkies began a nodding-out dance, a combination of Indian movements intermingled with voodoo screams. The cops, still mesmerized by the exposed breasts with needles sticking into them and the nipples bound with electronic tape, began consulting their rules book, trying to find a New York City law that was being defiled. Several well-dressed pedestrians stopped to observe this dazzling display of street art. They were probably professors of anthropology.

"Let's do it," Rick whispered, his hot tongue in Rosie's ear.

"No way."

"I thought you were a liberated lady."

"Nobody's that liberated."

"We've gotten it on in the park before."

"Not in punk dress. Those cops will arrest us in a second. And they'll throw away the key."

"Well, if I can't have you, I'm thirsty," Rick teased.

"Let's get a Coke. There's a pizza place across the street."

"Okay, but remember, after we deliver Angelique safely home, we're not staying for ravioli."

"Why not, handsome?"

"Because I have something better to fill you up with." Rick flirted outrageously. Rosie giggled and kissed him.

"It's a date."

Hand in hand, trying to look normal, they skipped across the street. As they approached the pizza place, a crowd of little girls carrying ballet totes erupted into the street.

"The concert must be over," Rosie observed.

Rick turned quickly. Suddenly, two men appeared behind them. Rick picked Rosie up and spun her through the doors of the pizza parlor before she could protest. One man got Rick in the groin with his knee. The other grabbed his face with two stiff thumbs, which caused Rick's head to jerk savagely. The girls began screaming as pain filled Rick's body. He tried to turn, but both men had a tight grip and he could not get free. He shut his eyes and concentrated. Abruptly, he fell back against them, causing them to fall off balance. Behind him, he heard Rosie's screams. He turned, concerned for her safety, when a man slammed him. Rick slammed him back, hard against the brick wall. Suddenly, the fight went out of the stranger. Then something crushed Rick's face. The pain was very sharp, but the sound was more terrible. "Miserable faggot," the attacker said. Rick lunged and slammed the man with all his strength. The blow was hard enough to drive his attacker back to the curb. Stunned, the man reached into his pocket. Quickly, Rick kicked him hard in the face. The man buckled, clinging wildly to the lip fragments with his left hand. His eye blew up suddenly and blood erupted from one ear.

"Ricky, behind you." Rosie shouted.

Rick turned but he wasn't quick enough. A third attacker struck him with enough force so that Rick lost his balance. But quickly he regained his bearing, using his elbow for leverage, and karate-chopped the man right off the sidewalk. Then Rick ran after him and put his hands around his throat. He began choking him and blood splurted voluminously into Rick's face. The man fell as Rick let his grip go. The smell of blood caused Rick to feel faint. The last thing he remembered was wondering whether Rosie was safe.

"Rick, are you dead?" he heard her ask when he regained consciousness.

He opened his eyes. "Don't think so."

"Are you sure you're not dead?" She'd been crying and the punk makeup streaked her face grotesquely.

"What happened?"

"You beat the beasts to a pulp," she said proudly. "Come on, we've got to get Angelique out of here."

Suddenly, the girl screamed. "Rick! Help me!"

"Not so fast." Vito Borgotta's voice was ominous.

"Help her!" Rosie screamed to the spectators. Nobody moved.

Rick scrambled to his feet. "You can't!" he shouted.

But Vito was too fast for Rick. He held onto Angelique, his Paul Newman blue eyes blazing with passion. Then they both disappeared into a long black car, which sped down Waverly Place and out of sight.

23

The grounds of the Asbury Park palazzo resembled an armed fortress during medieval times. Two rows of men flanked the protective walls that separated Don Vito's estate from the rest of the world. Louie the Lip and Aldo the Arm, two of Borgotta's inner circle, regularly checked the guards. They were doing this not only for security reasons, but for psychological support. Louie and Aldo tried to reassure the men that Don Vito was temporarily indisposed due to an affair of the heart. The men knew that their leader was a passionate man, who, for the sake of love, could lose all good sense. During these times, Louie and Aldo took over the running of the family. All business transactions were successfully commanded. No one was really worried, for daily profits were lucrative enough to assure loyalty. And the men knew that during his passionate affairs, the don would reward loyalty with huge bonuses.

They shared only one wish: that the Council would not hear about Don Vito's latest affair until it had normalized.

It had happened before. The passions of the heart were not unknown among the Council's circles. When dons had let personal desires interfere with business, they were retired gracefully. This retirement came in many forms. A choice to return to Sicily. A choice to be murdered. A choice to die naturally. The Council was strict in observing business first, personal affairs second. Don Vito was a severe observer of the Council's rule, except during his love phases. That's why Louie and Aldo were worried.

They checked security again. Everything seemed airtight. They checked the second floor bedroom window, beyond which Vito was pressing for Angelique's love. The Council would be furious if they knew that Vito had kidnapped a girl who was only thirteen. Besides, she was the daughter of the Salernos, whom Vito was suspected of eliminating. To complicate matters further, upstairs, in the master bedroom, Vito's possessive wife, Filomena, was handcuffed to her bed. Like most insane women, Filomena experienced inexplicable psychic renderings of Vito's actions. That's why, though she was carefully watched by a nurse, the men were uncomfortable. Suppose Filomena discovered that Vito had fallen passionately in love again? It had happened before and some even suspected that Filomena had been responsible for the Salernos' murders. Perhaps someone from her family did it? Louie and Aldo knew nothing about the severed hands affair except what they read in the papers. But the murderer could be anyone who knew Don Vito. The don dominated every man and woman he knew. Poor Angelique. What did Vito want from the young girl? Louie and Aldo tried not to think about this because Angelique was underage. If the Council heard, Don Vito would be retired, one way or the other.

In the second-floor bedroom, Angelique was still dressed in her sky-blue leotard. At thirteen, the promise of womanhood was budding. Vito was mesmerized by the sensuality of the young virgin. She searched his face for a hint of his intentions. Her oval-shaped eyes were troubled. Her fair skin darkened with the blush of raw emotion. Her mouth was rich as she smiled at him sweetly. She had no idea why she'd been brought to the palazzo, but assumed it was about her safety. Uncle Vito had been terribly kind since her parents' sudden death. He'd visited her, repeating often that he had respected her family. Angelique had heard the rumors that Vito had passionately loved her mother. But her mother was extremely beautiful and many men had loved her. Her father had told Angelique that a beautiful woman could remain faithful to her husband, even though many men desired her. Angelique believed him and was unaware that Vito had been her mother's lover. And she was apprehensive now, because Rick and Rosie had hidden her from Vito, but she tried to hide her anxiety.

"Uncle Vito, do I have to stay here?" she asked.

"You will be safer."

"May I call Aunt Anita?"

"Not right now."

"Does she know where I am?"

"Yes, she does," he lied.

"How long will I have to stay here?"

"Angelique, I'd like you to live here with me. Would you like that?"

He seemed different and she suddenly felt nervous. "But my ballet lessons. And my friends. And my family . . ." she began.

"You could have all of that here. I would hire the finest ballet teacher for you. We could convert a guest room into a private studio. Your friends could visit you. Your family. Just think, you wouldn't ever have to leave here."

"I want to go home."

"First, we'll take a trip," he continued, not heeding her request. He sat next to her on the sofa. "We'll go to Venice. Think of it. We'll ride in gondolas. Then we'll fly to Paris and London. They have wonderful ballet companies."

As he spoke, he patted her hands. She felt uncomfortable, for his hands were sweaty. Gracefully, she pulled away.

"I don't think so," she said.

Vito grew impatient. He was used to women saying yes to his requests. He knew he had a strange influence over others, a hypnotic effect. It had worked with everyone he wanted. But he was forgetting Angelique's age.

Vito whispered endearments into Angelique's ear. Blushing furiously, she leapt off the sofa. Something deep within Vito was hurt by her refusal. But he shook these awesome feelings away. He had to keep his wits about him. All his life he had won every woman he'd wanted. There hadn't been many. But he loved each one completely. He'd risked everything for them. And they had risked everything for him.

But, after all, that was love.

His passionate heart began beating rapidly. A man in his position did not have to be vulnerable but, Vito continually forced himself to be so, for he believed that love should flourish from the body to the soul. And he wanted Angelique's soul as well as her body.

"Angelique," he whispered. "Why won't you travel to Europe with me?"

"Why don't you take your wife?" she replied with SoHo street smarts.

He cringed under her sudden hostility. "Filomena is very ill."

"Is that why you pursued my mother?"

"I loved your mother. She was a saint."

"Did you kill her? Everybody says you did." Angelique felt an irresistible anger. "I didn't believe it was possible before."

"I swear on the Madonna that I had nothing to do with your parents' deaths."

"I don't believe you."

"I will find the murderer. I promise. And when I do, I'll punish him."

Vito was sure that Sally and Tony's murder was a business decision on the part of his enemies. Who, he did not know yet.

"Uncle Vito, please send me home."

"I cannot do that."

Feeling deep anguish, Vito walked over to the window, where he viewed the men guarding his estate. He observed that several men had removed their jackets in the heat. He would reprimand them. Vito insisted that everything should be orderly and proper. He walked back to Angelique and sat next to her. Gently, he put his arm around her shoulders. But the girl moved away. Vito's body shuddered with violent desire. He felt as if he were dying inside. Her beauty accelerated his heartbeats. She was in the first bloom of sensuality and Vito did not want anyone else to pluck her sweet innocence. He had loved Sally passionately and he'd lost her. He could not afford to lose Angelique. If he did, he would not be able to go on.

Love was Vito's curse, for he was not like other men. He never loved casually. He courted each woman as if he'd never known love before. When his lover returned his passion, Vito would nurture her. He taught his love everything he knew, in bed and out of bed. Every woman in his life had ended up adoring him. He'd cultivated each affair slowly, like a rare rose garden. And he was never sorry. For in the end, he was rewarded with loyalty and reverence, as no other man had ever been.

"Please," Angelique pleaded. Frightened, she backed away from him. Vito closed his eyes. Yes, she looked like a war orphan now. The fear in her face transformed her. World War II was Vito's favorite period. Often, he played war games in the bedroom, where he liked to fantasize being a Nazi general in a concentration camp.

"You must learn to trust me, dear," he commanded.

She began weeping.

"We will travel as uncle and niece."

"But you're not my real uncle," she sobbed.

"Angelique, don't say that. It pains me."

He forced her into his arms.

"Angelique, don't torture me," he groaned. Her body scent heightened his passion. It could not be duplicated by perfume, no matter how expensive. He drew her closer. She trembled. He reached for the drapery cord. When he pulled it, the drapes completely covered the windows and plunged the room into darkness. Vito pressed his throbbing body upon Angelique. She tried to fight him, but his control was impenetrable. They fell from the sofa onto the deep plush rug. Vito's hold filled Angelique with unbearable fright. Finally, she screamed.

"Don't be frightened, my little bird," he cooed as his hand explored her body. He tried to blot out her incredible, shattering screams. Instead, he focused on her flesh, warming her with his insistent yet tender touch. He knew how to change a woman's body warmth and knew that afterward, she would feel desire for him. But he forgot that Angelique was not a woman but a girl. Terrified, she continued to scream.

Suddenly, someone was in the doorway.

"Get out," Vito shouted.

But a woman raged into the dark room.

"Filomena!" Vito screamed as he rose from the floor. But the attacker was too fast for him and kicked Vito in the head, causing temporary visual confusion. Then he heard Angelique scream in terror. Vito focused and saw two hands around the girl's throat. He struggled to unclamp each finger. Then he pushed the attacker away from the girl. In her fright, Angelique pushed past Vito and he lost his balance. The attacker broke free. She raised her hand. In the darkness, something glinted as she lunged for Angelique. Instinctively the girl moved away. But she was not quick enough. Suddenly, she screamed with unbearable pain. Vito ran to Angelique as her attacker disappeared. Horrified, he saw Angelique's thumb, which had been hacked off and was lying on the plush gold carpet. Angelique screamed again. Vito rushed to her side and saw that the girl was covered with blood.

24

The men sitting at the table were gaunt and gray, as if a lifetime of waging war against society had robbed them of their natural color. What a contrast to their immigrant forebears, who, ruddy-faced and strong-bodied, had arrived in America to search for fame and fortune. A few of these pioneers were still in the Council. In any other business, these old-timers would have been retired. But there was no retirement here; besides, age and experience conveyed true wisdom, which was respected by all, even the young turks who wanted to take control.

The East Coast Council was seated at the long narrow table, surrounded by younger assistants. The young group had tailored their image to contrast with Hollywood's version of gangsters. All were dressed by European tailors of renown.

This was an important meeting, for one of the Council was in disgrace, serious business in the brutal struggle for power that the organization was embarked on. For the last twenty years, the Council had issued strict orders that members convert from illegal to legal activities. The younger element had convinced the old dons that legality was as profitable, if done in the American way. The old style went out of fashion. No more *High Noon*s. Headlines were avoided at extravagant costs to all. When rubout exercises were necessary, they were accomplished with no fanfare and, certainly, no publicity. The dons wanted their grandchildren to grow up in the prosperous American culture and take their place in the world of business, politics, and society. Everyone agreed that the old ways had outlived their usefulness. For twenty years, this had been orchestrated perfectly. But the rooftop murders had destroyed all these years of accomplishment. Before them now was Vito Borgotta, who was personally responsible for this mess.

Standing in front of his peers, Don Vito looked All-American. He'd always been different from the others. He'd risen to the Council at a younger age than anyone in the Organization's history. He was admired because he was unlike his hot-blooded colleagues. Vito was noted for his cool assessment of controversial matters and was one of the pioneers of this current philosophy of avoiding murder, mayhem, and the media.

But Vito had one flaw. When in love, Vito was as hot-blooded as any raw recruit from Sicily. The only thing that had saved his career was that Vito did not fall in love often.

The oldest don at the table, Don Cicillini from Brooklyn, fingered a long Cuban cigar he wasn't supposed to smoke. Suffering from throat cancer, the don's voice caused others to tremble.

"Some people think you've let your personal business interfere with our business. This has caused a lot of trouble, Don Vito. We can't take the heat for you."

"I've always come through," Vito answered with a coolly superior air that was not missed by the Council members. "My receipts alone assure that I am the front-runner in our gambling ventures."

"Don Vito, we are not quarreling with your receipts. We are quarreling with the trouble you've caused us."

All Council members nodded in agreement.

"My family has always honored its commitment to the Council," Vito insisted.

"We know that, Don Vito." The speaker was Don Sprinoza from the Bronx, a slim man with a nervous tick. The tick made it impossible to forecast when he would decide to reach for his gun. Over the years, this tick had served Don Sprinoza very well. "I have taken up gardening. Do you know why?" Don Sprinoza did not hesitate to continue. "Gardening teaches a man patience. And a man needs patience when he is building for his family. Don't you agree?"

"Your patience has paid off, Don Sprinoza," Vito replied. "Your roses were beautiful."

Vito was furious at being summoned before the Council without warning. Early that morning, six dozen roses, formed into a bleeding heart shape, had arrived at the palazzo gate. The men who delivered the roses had waited for Vito to respond to the calling card of the Council. Vito had not wanted to leave Angelique, but he had no choice. He left his two trusted men, Aldo and Louie, guarding the girl. He'd summoned his personal physician, Dr. Calami, to tend to the girl's injury. Vito had been dismayed to learn that Angelique's thumb could not be replaced because no one had thought to ice-pack it. The thumb had lain on the plush carpet while Vito had tried to comfort Angelique.

The roses had arrived at a most inopportune time. Angelique had been given a sedative and was finally asleep; the doctor had cleaned and bandaged the place of the amputation. Vito had been on his way to question his wife's nurse when he was informed about the delivery of roses. He'd had to obey. To disobey would have meant immediate death. Quickly, he left for the Atlantic City meeting, hoping that his estate, his wife, and Angelique would be well guarded from danger.

Now, as he stood alone before the banquet table, Vito was filled with resentment. He knew he was hard boiled in every way but one. Yet his one weakness would probably finish him off. Zealously, he examined the faces of his colleagues. Yes, they were out for his blood. He knew they would use this personal problem for their own greedy ends.

His business was one of the most lucrative and had been envied by most of them. Well, they were about to make their move.

To the unfamiliar eye, the meeting did not look serious. Food was plentiful, wine bottles littered the table, and clouds of cigar smoke filled the room. But Vito kept his attention on his colleagues' expression, vowing to survive for Angelique and their future together.

"You have been brought here," Don Francesco from Boston said, "because you have broken the rules." He chomped on his cigar dramatically. "You have brought the headlines upon us. You know this is what we wanted to avoid because of our new business ventures."

"I had nothing to do with the rooftop murders," Vito declared.

Guffaws and shrugs went around the table. Vito stared ahead, his blue eyes clear and icy cold.

"I repeat. I had nothing to do with the murders."

"Then who killed the Salernos?" Don Francesco inquired.

"I have no idea."

"Are you saying that you did not rub out Sally and Tony?" Don Sprinoza accused.

"That is exactly what I am saying."

"But this is impossible to believe. Besides, we know your wife comes from Gelenta and her family is still there."

"What has my wife to do with this?"

"It is known that in Gelenta, when someone is a cuckold, the hands of the guilty party are severed to mark the infidelity. Isn't this so?"

"I believe so."

"Don't you think it is an odd coincidence that the hands of Tony and Sally Salerno were severed before they were killed?"

"My wife is ill. She never leaves her bedroom."

"We are sympathetic to your wife's illness, yet we have been informed that only yesterday, someone was attacked in your house. Did your wife do that?"

Vito swore under his breath. One of his men was a snitch. "I demand that my private business remain personal."

"Normally, we would grant this wish," Don Cicillini said. "But in this case you have made your personal business part of our business. Remember, we are businessmen. We are not animals, are we?" All agreed. "But you have been acting like a crazed animal. For instance, is it not the action of an animal to kidnap Angelique Salerno?"

"I did not kidnap her. I merely wished to place her under my protection. Whoever killed her parents might want to harm the girl, too."

"But we believe you have placed the girl in jeopardy."

"What do you mean?"

"She's in your home, isn't she? And she has been injured, hasn't she? We believe that whoever was responsible for those murders lives in your house. Was it you? Your wife? One of your men? What will happen when the newspapers discover this? We will all look like animals, won't we? And everything we have accomplished for our families will be washed away." Don Cicillini paused. "You are aware of the ways Americans insult us. My own daughter had a terrible time getting my grandchildren in prep school because of their name. Is it fair that my grandchildren should suffer because you cannot control your animal passions, Don Vito?"

Deep within him, Vito's spirit collapsed. He knew the signs. The Council had already decided his punishment. But he would play out his role until the last moment.

"What do you want?"

"Go on a trip. Visit Sicily. Relax. Drink wine. Eat cheese. Sleep all day. We will take care of your business."

"How will you do that?"

"We will place a substitute in your spot. When you return, you will feel better. Your wife will feel better. Everyone will feel better. Especially us."

Vito knew he was being forcibly removed from the Council. He had two choices. Either he obeyed or he would be killed. Of course, they might kill him even if he obeyed.

"I don't think I can do that."

"Don Vito, we forgave you for your unreasonable passions before. Do you remember?"

Vito was silent.

"Remember all the trouble you caused when Irene Muncilli married into the Caesare family?"

Vito nodded.

"You were young and we forgave you. We are not unreasonable men, you see."

Vito nodded again.

"And we will forgive you again, if you do as we wish."

Vito knew there was no escape.

"As you wish," he said grimly.

"Good, Don Vito. I'm glad you have decided to be sensible about this." Don Cicillini smiled benignly. "Now, join us. Sit next to me." He pointed to an empty chair. "Relax. Come." He waved to Vito.

Hesitantly, Vito joined the men at the table. They smiled at him, inviting him to enjoy the food and drink. But Vito kept cool. He thought, there is only one matter of substance in this world, and that is the issue of life and death. Everything else is trivial, especially love. He knew that now.

25

The armed sentries at the palazzo were itchy. Don Vito had been gone for twenty-four hours and there had been no word through the usual sources. Louie the Lip and Aldo the Arm had not slept because the don's wife had been noisier than usual. The nurse said that Filomena had demanded to see her husband. Dr. Calami had given the half-crazed woman several injections. Half the time she didn't know what she was saying or doing. Because he was Vito's personal physician, Dr. Calami was used to tending serious wounds without the benefit of hospitals. When he checked on Angelique's wound, the young girl begged permission to call home, but Louie and Aldo refused. Don Vito would have to make all decisions regarding Angelique. But they were worried. The guards had been thoroughly trained for times when endurance was more important than battle. Vito had benefited from his study of the Roman Era. But Asbury Park was scorching and the men's patience was fraying. Their apprehension focused on Vito.

Where was the don?

What was going to happen?

It had been a hot night and at sunrise, the bursting sun promised no relief for the day. At seven A.M., when a dark blue car was sighted, Louie and Aldo were called to the gates.

Slowly the car careened down the private road that led to the estate. All the men waited at attention, shotguns ready. Though they knew nothing could break through the electronically locked gates, they were prepared for anything. The blue car continued down the road, turning quickly and speeding up at the gates. Then it reversed, turned around, and drove away. The men relaxed, assuming the driver had been lost. They watched the car disappear. One of them sighted a black plastic bag on the road.

Cautiously, the gates were unlocked and two men carried the black plastic bag into the grounds. Quickly, they locked the gates behind them. The men carried the bag to the back terrace, where Louie and Aldo opened it. They swore when they saw the contents. Inside the bag was Vito's naked body. They swore again when they discovered that Vito had been deprived of his manhood, a mark of the Council's extreme anger.

"Bury him in the garden quick," Louie hissed. "And keep this quiet. We don't want it to get out. Not yet."

Instantly, the men followed orders. As they executed their task, the curtains of Filomena's windows moved. Fearing Filomena's interference, Louie and Aldo ran upstairs to the back bedroom where Angelique was resting.

"Listen, we're going to get you out of this place," Aldo promised. "You've got to move fast."

Angelique trembled as tears fell from her beautiful eyes. Though the doctor had given her pain killers, her hand was throbbing. Every time she looked at her thumb bandage, she burst into tears. She was disfigured. Her future was destroyed. A ballet dancer needed all ten fingers to project the grace and beauty of a fine performance. Angelique had asked Dr. Calami whether plastic surgery could be used to replace her thumb, and he had said there was a chance.

"Come on, doll. We're trying to save your life," Louie hissed.

Panicked, Angelique and the men ran. At the rear door, they hopped into a car. After a half-hour on the New Jersey

Turnpike, Louie and Aldo planned their next move. They knew the Council would take control of Vito's business and kill his confidants. Aldo and Louie formed a plan to parley for their lives, and Angelique was the bait.

"Where're we going?" Angelique asked.

"You'll be home soon," Aldo replied. "Louie, stop at that gas station. I want to make a phone call."

In the booth, he filled the phone with coins.

Crazy Nuz was cooking pizzas when the phone rang at the club.

"Yeah?" he answered.

"Who's this?" Aldo asked.

"Nobody," Nuz answered. But he recognized Aldo's voice.

"Look, I want to talk to somebody."

"What about?"

"Nuz?" Aldo recognized the distinct tones of Nuz's rasping voice. "Look, Nuz. We got the girl. We'll trade her for clemency. Okay?"

"I can't answer for that."

"Nuz. Call the right people. Make a deal."

"They'll want to know whether the girl is okay. Is she?"

"Vito didn't touch her."

"Are you sure?"

"She only had a slight accident."

"Where?" Nuz demanded, knowing that a virgin was worth more than a non-virgin in any swap.

"It had nothing to do with that."

"Where did she have the accident?" Nuz again insisted.

There was a long silence.

"Her face?" Nuz asked.

"No."

"Then where?"

"Her thumb."

"Her what?"

"Her thumb. You know, on her hand."

"Jesus, another hand!" Nuz swore.

"It isn't serious, Nuz."

"I'll pass the word along. Call me back in two hours."

Nuz slammed down the phone. At the other end, Aldo swore. Then he ran into the men's toilet, where he suffered from extreme diarrhea.

When he returned to the car, Louie yelled, "You took your time."

"We have to call back in two hours."

"Where should we go?"

"To the city."

"They might look for us there."

"We'll go uptown. They'll never look for us there."

"Can't you take me home?" Angelique asked meekly.

"No, doll. They'll be watching your aunt's apartment."

"Can you take me to Rosie Caesare's?"

"Mario's kid. Naw. He'll explode if we do that. Don't worry, doll. We'll get you back home safe and sound."

Two hours later they were circling Lincoln Center. Aldo called Crazy Nuz to learn that he and Louie would not be killed if Angelique was returned unharmed. But Nuz said that Angelique should temporarily stay out of SoHo and gave them a safe place to stash her.

When he returned to the car, Aldo told Louie to drive down 57th Street.

"Why Fifty-seventh Street? We don't know nobody there," Louie protested as he turned into the wide avenue.

"We're dropping off the doll."

"Who does she know on Fifty-seventh Street?"

"Nobody. Crazy Nuz told me where to take her. Stop at that brown building."

Louie stopped the car. Aldo opened the door for Angelique.

"I'll be right back, Louie. Come on, doll."

"Where're you taking me?"

"To Miles Hamilton."

"I don't know any Miles Hamilton."

"He's a friend of Rosie's."

Angelique knew that 57th Street was Rosie's favorite street, so it made sense that Rosie would have a friend there. She followed Aldo into the tall building. When they arrived on the sixth floor, they found a receptionist who looked like Linda Evans.

"May I help you?" she asked.

"We got a package for Miles Hamilton," Aldo hissed.

She looked at him, then shrugged her shoulders as she buzzed Hamilton. Because Miles was a literary agent, all of his friends looked strange to her.

"Tell Mr. Hamilton there's a package for him, okay?" the receptionist said into the phone. Then she said to Angelique, "Through those doors and turn right."

As Angelique followed directions, Aldo disappeared. When she saw a dust jacket of Rosie's novel *Sweet Dreamdust* hanging on a wall, Angelique felt safe.

"Hello," a vibrant man greeted her. "I'm Rosie's literary agent. You're Angelique?"

"Yes."

"Rosie asked me to look after you."

"Thank you very much," Angelique said politely. "Can you tell me why?"

"I'm not at liberty to say, but I think it has something to do with the New York City Police Department and those other people."

Angelique nodded. Obviously, things were still dangerous downtown. She settled into a comfortable chair next to a pile of magazines. As she skimmed the pages of *People*, she meditated on how important a thumb was.

26

The slim woman in the dark hat was standing in the doorway of a SoHo loft building. The old structure was being converted into a condominium complex, but at night the site was abandoned. Broadway was very dark and she could see lights burning clearly in Rosie's loft. Patiently, the woman waited. Her next decisions were most important because they would make sense of her entire life. Funny how things came to that. One action could insure a place in history. She smiled. They would write about her and try to analyze her motives. What would they call her? A mad woman? But she was not mad. Simply put, she was cut from the cloth of the past, when women knew how to love men. There had been many famous women like herself. Her favorite was Joan of Arc, who died for passion. She'd read everything written about the Saint. Though the Church announced that Joan had died for God, the woman didn't agree. She knew that the Church and the State always revised history to suit their aims. No, Joan burned because she believed passionately in her destiny. The pure of spirit were always killed by the weak ones. The woman felt her fury rise when she thought of what had been done to her lover. How dare they touch him! How dare they maim him! What an insult to his memory. She'd come into the garden as his men were burying his body. She'd held onto him closely, wanting to breathe life back into him, but it was too late.

Yet he had prepared her for this. They had often talked about fate. A man must submit to his fate, he'd said. Of course, she had planned his fate differently. She'd arranged for them to live quietly, hidden in the Austrian mountains. She'd planned everything, even down to the unnumbered Swiss Bank accounts.

But Vito had hesitated, because of that girl.

She'd warned that he was running his luck too long. Sooner or later the Council would move against him. But he had not listened to her.

After she'd held his dead body, she'd pulled at the stubs of her shaven head, trying to inflect self-injury. Then she'd stopped. If anyone should be punished, it certainly was not her. There were others. And she would personally see to it. First, the young girl, Angelique. Then that reporter and her husband. They would be easy to kill for they did not believe in the old ways. Vito had taught them to her, explaining that they were the best way to surprise victims. Wait first. Then strike without warning. After these three were dead, she would begin on the Caesare family. After that, she would eliminate the Council. But this would be treacherous work. They knew about the old ways of the primitive.

Her heartbeats were rapid. No, it would not do to surrender to her fury now. It was too soon. She had to remain strong for Vito. She had to avenge his death. She would wait until everyone thought life was safe again. She would strike at the perfect moment.

Six weeks had passed and the police were still searching for Filomena Borgotta. They wanted to question Vito's widow about the strange coincidences of Gelenta's severed-hands customs and the rooftop murders. Detective Kushel had finally uncovered this information and it had changed his perspective on the case. Rumors spread throughout SoHo that Filomena had been shipped back to Sicily by the Council. They had two important reasons for this action. First, they did not believe in killing women, and, second, Filomena's family could care for her. But no one knew exactly where Filomena was. Kushel had questioned everyone. When Angelique had suddenly appeared out of nowhere, she told Kushel that someone had tried to murder her. Who, she did not know. But that person had managed to sever her thumb. When pressed for more details, Angelique said that she could not remember anything after the attack. The next thing she knew, she was wandering the streets of SoHo with a bandaged hand. Kushel did not believe Angelique's story, but he could not refute it with hard evidence. Angelique's severed thumb piqued the detective. Though it was not the same as a whole severed hand, it was close enough to tie her into her parents' murder circumstancially. But why had only the girl's thumb been severed? Why not the whole hand? This mystery would be solved, Kushel thought, if he could locate Filomena. He pressed his snitches to ask questions, but the Italians had put a clamp on the whole issue. Everyone walked around with clenched lips. When he tried to question Angelique again, he discovered that she was in the hospital. Her doctor said that plastic surgery would be performed to try and give Angelique a thumb.

Meanwhile, Rosie kept writing and Rick kept revising, chapter by chapter. Miles read a part of the manuscript and complained that the book was turning into a passionate love story instead of a murder account. Rosie insisted that it was accurate, so Miles hastily informed her editor that Mafia romance would make as much money as Mafia murder. Hearing this, the editorial board at Bulloughs felt nervous. Would the public believe and sympathize with a murderer who fell madly in love with a married woman, and after she was severed and killed, fell madly in love with her daughter? Deep philosophical dialogues were forthcoming between the editorial staff and the sales staff. They came to the conclusion that if Angelique went on television to show her severed thumb, the book would be a best-seller. But Angelique was getting plastic surgery! Perhaps Rosie could talk her out of it, temporarily. When Miles presented this idea to Rosie, she nixed it. Miles was astonished. He knew how much Rosie wanted success. But Rosie said there was absolutely no way she would stand in Angelique's way of replacing the thumb. Besides, Angelique was still underage. When she became an adult, she could choose whether she wanted a place on television. Miles learned that there were some things Rosie would not do for fame. Promptly, he notified Bulloughs that this particular publicity campaign might not work. That sent the publishing staff back to pondering how best to break the book into today's headlines.

Rosie was writing fast.

"Hey, baby, I'm going for a run," Rick said to her one morning.

193

"Don't call me baby and don't interrupt me."

Rick left the loft. When Rosie was working, there was no reaching her.

From the doorway opposite the pink building, the slim woman in a dark hat saw Rick leave home for his daily run. For a month, she had clocked him and knew he would not return until afternoon. His wife generally worked until then. Good. That meant she was upstairs alone.

After Angelique had returned home, Mario and Rick were always with Rosie and the girl. But as things quieted down, everyone relaxed. The cops had stopped following them as well. This was what the woman had waited for. Vito had taught her the values of patience and she had learned them well. Everyone would pay for Vito's death. She had a long list. Angelique was at the top, but the girl was in the hospital. So Rosie would take her place.

A few doors down, Rick stopped to talk to a tall, thin man. When Rick jogged away, the man entered the pink building. Quickly, the slim woman slipped into the doorway after him. Arnoldo looked at the stranger.

"What floor?" he asked politely.

"Three."

"The Ramseys? I don't know whether anyone is at home. Rick went out."

"I'm going to see his wife."

"Oh. She doesn't like to be disturbed when she's working. She's a holy terror. She hates me," Arnoldo babbled.

"It's okay. She expects me."

"All right. Here we go, up, up, up."

Arnoldo used his energy transport control. When the car reached three, he rang the Ramsey's doorbell. No one answered.

"See, I told you. She won't answer."

Immediately, the woman's karate chop felled Arnoldo. He lay unconscious, his tall, thin frame using up most of the elevator's floor. The woman picked the lock, another handy talent she'd learned from Vito. When the narrow door swung open, she saw that the loft was empty. She heard the click of a typewriter coming from behind a closed door. She opened her alligator bag and took out the cord, licking her lips in anticipation. It would be a slow and painful death. She crept closer to the door. But the phone rang and Rosie spoke to someone. The woman waited, impatient.

Arnoldo's vision was misty. What on earth had happened? He tried to sit up but couldn't move. His leg was broken. Who was that woman? Then, Arnoldo realized that she was probably going to harm Rosie. He reached around to his breast pocket where his verbal remote for the Princess robot was. He pressed a button and spoke to the robot.

Upstairs, in Arnoldo's loft, the Princess blinked. Then she marched over to the freight elevator and pressed the lobby button. Once downstairs, she glided out through the front door, causing a commotion on the street. She moved down Broadway until she reached the Pain Shop. Then she marched into the place. Arnoldo knew Rick was there.

"Chuggg Byrrrr," the Princess said to Rick.

"Arnoldo's playing games again," Rick said to the shop's owner, Montana Smiley.

"Looks like she's trying to tell you something, Rick."

"Oh, Arnoldo's crazy," Rick replied.

"But, Rick. Isn't Rosie up there alone? Maybe . . ."

He was out the doorway before Montana could finish her sentence. When he saw that the elevator had stopped on the third floor, he got worried. Quickly, he ran up the fire escape. Then he quietly let himself into the loft by the rear door.

"Okay, Miles. See you tomorrow for lunch," Rosie said.

The slim woman spun the cord tightly about her fists. Slowly, she pushed open the bedroom door. Rosie was hunched over her typewriter, intent on her next words, oblivious to the world. The woman crept forward. Suddenly, Rosie turned, surprising the attacker. Startled, Rosie lost her balance as her typing chair overturned. The woman pounced, but lost her bearings. She tried to draw the cord around Rosie's neck, but Rosie struggled too hard. Rosie screamed. The woman karate-chopped Rosie on the chin and Rosie fell in a dead faint. Then the woman began encircling Rosie's neck with the cord. But she felt something. Suddenly, she turned. In the doorway, Rick stood, watching.

Rick reacted with shock. Before him, Filomena Borgotta's nurse was about to strangle his wife. She moved swiftly and kicked Rick. He doubled over. He hit the floor, next to Rosie. Was she dead? The nurse kicked Rick in his face. A bomb exploded. Two teeth caught in his throat. He coughed them up, gasping for breath. His eyes were swelling like balloons. He was losing control of his body. Then the woman battered him again. Something must have been severed, for Rick could see only blood. He forced his swollen eyes open. Through the red maze, he saw the cord in the nurse's hands as she whipped it around his throat.

My God, he thought, she's going to kill me. Instantly, he reacted, every movement oozing blood. He grabbed one of her hands. The nurse struggled to free it, but Rick held onto it with all his strength. She was like a cobra, twisting and turning, ready to strike. Rick bent her hand backward, but she was too strong and broke free. Then he twisted around as she kicked him in the genitals and he fell in pain. From the floor, he looked up at her. He quivered with fear at what he saw. Her hat had fallen to the ground and she stood there with bulging eyes filled with hate, eyes that protruded from her shaven head like two swollen snakes.

"You're a dead man," she hissed as she swung at him with her lethal foot.

Swiftly, he reacted and she did not expect it. He raised his feet and clamped them about her thighs in a stranglehold. Then he squeezed with all his strength. It worked. She dropped the cord and fell backward. He thought she was out and slackened his hold, but she whipped about, surprising him. He ducked in time and she missed. Rick took advantage of this to twist both arms backward. Then he held her prisoner, backing her against the wall, praying that she'd quit. But she wouldn't. She raised her foot. She kicked him in the genitals again and he bent over in extreme pain.

"You killed the only man I loved," she hissed.

"I didn't kill anybody," he screamed.

"You're going to die," she whispered, her strange eyes filled with evil.

My God, he thought, she won't quit. What am I going to do? I can't kill a woman.

Rick felt faint as the nurse kicked him again and again. Blood gushed everywhere. He was dizzy. He tried to focus, but the pounding in his head was making it impossible. Then it occurred to him that she was not only determined to kill him, but after his demise, she would kill Rosie.

No, he thought. That can't happen. Not my Rosie.

His blood rushed through his head in an agonizing surge of strength. He broke away from her clamp on his body. In an effort of supreme will, he pinned her arms down again. But her feet were still lethal weapons. He twisted her body, then encircled her legs with a leg lock. They both fell to the ground. The nurse hissed and spat in his face. Quickly, she spun to free herself. This time Rick was ready. As she spun away from him, he reached out for the cord. Then he wove it around her neck. The cord pulled at her throat, choking off her breath. Her face turned purple. Suddenly, she was no longer in control of her body. Her legs folded under her. She fell to the floor again, next to Rick. He drew the cord tighter and watched it cut into her flesh. Her eyes bulged as if in ecstasy. Then she opened her mouth and blood gushed out. Feeling faint-hearted, Rick steeled himself not to lose his grasp. Again, he tightened the cord, watching with horror as her body erupted with urine.

28

The headlines screamed across the country: PRIME SUSPECT IN ROOFTOP MURDERS—NURSE TRIES TO KILL REPORTERS. Bulloughs Publishing was ecstatic about the publicity and sent dozens of red roses to Rick and Rosie's loft. Miles called to say that the movie people were definitely going ahead with the film. Detective Kushel dropped by to tell Rick and Rosie that he could definitely prove that the nurse was the murderer of Tony and Sally Salerno. Apparently, the nurse had kept a record of her love-obsessed activities.

"You know, darling," Rosie said as they held hands, sitting in a street café, "if we could get our hands on the nurse's diary, it would be great for our book."

"Maybe we can sue under the Freedom of Information Act?"

"Darling, you're mighty smart."

But Rick wasn't feeling intelligent. Rather, he was depressed, although everyone told him he'd done the right thing. How could killing be right? No, he could never condone the taking of another person's life.

Mario had tried to comfort Rick. "Hey, kid. Sometimes we gotta do things that are against our beliefs and our nature. That babe killed two people already. She would have killed you and Rosie without a thought. Then she would have gotten Angelique. She was crazy in love with Vito. A woman like that is bananas."

"Rick, are you still feeling depressed?" Rosie squeezed his hand.

"Rosie, it seems the longer I live, the more macho I become."

"That's not so. You're a wonderful man and I love you."

"Do you?"

"Yes, I do. And, remember, murder is not sexist. Anyone can do it."

"Rosie, because of the murder, I know something I didn't know before."

"What's that, honey?"

"That life is simple and complicated at the same time."

"How do you mean?"

"It's the same. Life and death. Love and hate. They're alike. You find that out in a crisis when things become black and white, like it did with the nurse. I knew if I didn't kill her, she would have killed me." He paused. "But day to day, we don't live in a crisis, so we muddle up things."

"To most people, life is always a muddle, Rick."

"Not to you. You live on the raw edges. That's why I fell in love with you when you were only fourteen."

"Honest?"

"Rosie, you were the first really decisive person I'd ever met. Everyone else in my world was gray. My mother was light gray. My father was dark gray. But you were bright yellow with a center of fierce red."

"And what color are you?" she laughed.

"Maybe a budding blue?"

"I think you're definitely a royal purple."

"Honey," he said, "let's go home and finish the book. No more running around in circles for me. On to the color purple."

"That's my guy!"

She blew him a warm kiss as a group of young girls

dressed in navy-blue jackets and plaid skirts passed the café. It was the beginning of the fall school term and the teenage girls were oblivious to everything except one another. They were screaming, comparing lipsticks, nail polish, shoes, hairstyles. The summer had separated them and they had lots to catch up on about boys, rock stars, and TV videos. The girls came in all sizes and shapes, but most had dark brown hair and eyes, and the lovely wide smiles of children of Italian blood. In the midst of the group was Angelique. Her hand was still bandaged and she had dark circles under her eyes, but the rest of her face reflected the kind of joy that a young girl should feel. When she saw Rick and Rosie sitting at the café, dressed in their SoHo attire, Angelique waved. Her pals stared at this infamous avant-garde couple. They asked Angelique questions. Were Rick and Rosie really going to be on television? Had Rosie really grown up in SoHo? Had she really written books? Angelique nodded to these queries. Her pals giggled with excitement, wondering at the limitless possibilities of their future. They walked on slowly, the future inviting them to dream. Suddenly, Angelique broke from the pack and ran to the café. Impulsively, she planted a warm kiss on Rick's cheek.

"Thanks for saving my life," she said.

Then she flung her arms around Rosie.

"Go for it, Angelique," Rosie whispered.